CLAIRE'S LAST SECRET

CLAIRE'S LAST SECRET

Marty Ambrose

Severn House

This first world edition published 2018
in Great Britain and the USA by
SEVERN HOUSE PUBLISHERS LTD of
Eardley House, 4 Uxbridge Street, London W8 7SY.
Trade paperback edition first published
in Great Britain and the USA 2018 by
SEVERN HOUSE PUBLISHERS LTD.

British Library Cataloguing in Publication Data
A CIP catalogue record for this title is available from the British Library.

ISBN-13: 978-0-7278-8797-9 (cased)
ISBN-13: 978-1-84751-919-1 (trade paper)
ISBN-13: 978-1-78010-975-6 (e-book)

All Severn House titles are printed on acid-free paper.

Severn House Publishers support the Forest Stewardship Council™ [FSC™],
the leading international forest certification organisation.
All our titles that are printed on FSC certified paper carry the FSC logo.

Typeset by Palimpsest Book Production Ltd.,
Falkirk, Stirlingshire, Scotland.
Printed and bound in Great Britain by
TJ International, Padstow, Cornwall.

For Jim – my hubby and best friend.

ACKNOWLEDGMENTS

This book has been the culmination of an amazing journey, and so many people helped me along the way. First of all, I want to thank the team at Florida SouthWestern State College who provided a grant for me to research the background of this novel in Geneva and Florence during the 200th anniversary of the 'haunted summer.' I never dreamed that I would actually see Mary Shelley's journal from 1816 or walk in the footsteps of the Byron/Shelley circle. From our president, Dr Allbritten, to Michelle Wright and Stella Egan, they were always supportive. But most of all, I want to express my appreciation to Susan Hibbard who spent many afternoons chatting with me, encouraging my travel and work – I am forever indebted to you, my friend. *Grazie mille.*

On the publishing side, I could not have found a home for this book without my incredible agent, Nicole Resciniti, who is just a gem in every way. Many thanks as well to the lovely people at Severn House: Kate Lyall Grant who wrote the most beautiful letter about my writing and Sara Porter who is one of the best editors with whom I have worked. Thanks to all of you for giving *Claire's Last Secret* a chance!

As always, my family has been there cheering me on – especially my husband, Jim McLaughlin, who endlessly read draft after draft of my chapters, bringing his journalist's red pen to my prose. Love you.

Lastly, I want to acknowledge the beautiful, mysterious, maddening Claire Clairmont, whose letters and life spoke to me through the centuries. I hope I did justice to your legacy.

'I am unhappily the victim of a happy passion. I had one; like all things perfect of its kind, it was fleeting, and mine only lasted ten minutes, but these ten minutes have discomposed the rest of my life . . .'

Claire Clairmont

ONE

H is letter came just at the point when I thought death was my only option.

Poverty had been creeping in like a shadow edging out the light, and it was only a matter of time before it engulfed what was left of my life and snuffed out any prospect that fate would offer another way. I could no longer envision a road that led to some lost yet cherished land of dreams – especially when I was too old to pick up and start over on some adventure that would lead me into a new dawn.

It was too late for that.

Those were the youthful regions where fortune bestowed some great, golden happiness on anyone who had the courage to live with soulful purpose – hardly the reality of my present circumstances.

Yet the letter brought a glimmer of hope . . . a wild fancy that I might, even at this late stage, turn things around. What I did not realize was that it would take me back to the early days and expose a labyrinth of deception and lies that had altered the course of my existence.

But I digress . . .

I must start at the beginning because the echoes of one's origin never fade to silence, no matter how much it is desired. I did not know my own origin because I never knew my father – not that I needed to learn his identity, but it would have centered my world at the very least with a starting point. A compass for my life. A moment when I first became aware that I drew breath.

Sadly, it never happened.

My last name is Clairmont. A melodic sobriquet to be sure, but my mother simply chose the name like someone would choose a ribbon for the bodice of a dress – it seemed appealing and created just the right effect of class and respectability – but it was for show, nonetheless, since she never married a man named Clairmont. Not that I particularly minded her choice. I love showiness. In my opinion, modesty in a woman is highly overrated, though no one in my family agreed with me. But I, Clara Mary Jane Clairmont, always went my own way – even without the compass – and I am prouder of that than of anything else in my seventy-five years on this earth.

Just as I claimed *my* version of my name: Claire Clairmont. *Il mio nome.*

'Aunt Claire, don't overtax yourself,' my niece, Paula, said as she strolled into the warm, slightly stuffy room, a cup of my favorite oolong tea in her hand. It was late morning – not terribly hot yet, but by afternoon the midsummer Florentine temperature would soar and everyone would take refuge inside, resting and praying to St Clare of Assisi for a breath of air. My rented apartment faced the Boboli Gardens – a lush, open space on the outskirts of Florence, perched on a hill, that often provided a slight breeze, whispering through the centuries-old cypress trees and hidden grottos.

Paula set a delicate blue-and-white patterned china cup on my tea table, already cluttered with letters, books, and an inkwell. 'You need to move around more, Aunt. Your ankle is starting to swell again, and if you cannot walk, I will have to call in Raphael to carry you to bed.' My niece's voice took on that familiar combination of love and exasperation of the young who are tethered to the old; she cared for me deeply, but I tried her patience when I refused to heed her advice, which occurred quite often. I wasn't ready to give up my independent ways yet.

Besides, she would not mind calling our *domestico*, Raphael; I'd seen the sweet longing in the glances that she cast at him when he was distracted by some task in the kitchen. Paula might be the daughter of my dearly departed brother, Charles, but she was also *my* niece, after all. Spinning romantic fantasies around a handsome face was embedded in her nature. Certainly, I had done that a time or two in my life – sometimes finding regret in my impulsive feelings, sometimes not. But always true to my passions.

Quickly, I slipped the letter under the stack of books, shifting in my chair and smoothing down my faded blue cotton dress. I was not ready to share it with her yet.

'Is that the missive you received this morning?' she asked absently, leaning down and plumping the delicately embroidered pillow under my sprained ankle, which was propped up on a footstool.

'Nothing important.' Assuming an air of nonchalance, I shrugged. 'Just a letter from one of my many old friends, Edward Trelawny, inquiring as to our well-being.'

Paula straightened with a sigh. 'Do we have *any* old friends left who have not abandoned us to our state of poverty, except Trelawny?'

'Thank you, my dear, for pointing that out. I am well aware of our impoverished state of affairs since my last ill-conceived investment in that farm.' Folding my wrinkled hands in my lap, I echoed her sigh. Investing in my nephew's farm in Austria was a foolishness that I could ill afford, but I never could resist helping my family, even though it had pushed me to the brink of bankruptcy.

'I apologize – that was unkind, Aunt.' She placed a hand on my forearm, glancing down at me with her blue eyes clouded in guilt.

'You are forgiven, even though I must remind you that friendships can ebb and flow during the years regardless of one's financial status – even those who are closest to us can disappoint us.' Of course, I meant the members of the sacred Byron/Shelley circle of my youth: Byron, the great poet who broke my heart, and Shelley, the husband of my stepsister, Mary, whose brilliance lit my life and whose small annuity protected me in my advanced years. I had loved them all – especially my accomplished and beautiful stepsister, Mary. Even though Mary had created a hideous monster in her novel *Frankenstein*, she herself possessed that kind of tranquil loveliness that made everyone gravitate to her.

Serenità, as the Italians would say.

Unlike me.

I could never sit still.

I talked incessantly.

And I never let my head rule my emotions, which caused me more heartache than I can say. But my life was never dull.

Geneva, Vienna, London, St Petersburg – I saw the world and I loved many men, though not always wisely.

'I have heard that Trelawny can barely read now his eyesight is so weak,' Paula said with a shake of her head. 'He is—'

'Old and decrepit? Like me?' I raised my brows, waiting for the truth to spill out of her. No one would deny that my once-glossy dark curls were now threaded with gray, my smooth olive skin had more than its share of wrinkles and my body experienced a variety of aches and pains. But my eyes still sparkled with the fires of my youth – just somewhat dimmed, from what I could see in the mirror. I knew all of that. Paula would not say it because, at heart, she had a fondness for me, and I had for her – and her young daughter, Georgiana. My niece and I were bonded in mutual affection and penury, but I refused to let the latter sink my spirits. 'In truth, I am quite ancient—'

'Hardly. You are only chair-bound because you twisted your ankle in the gardens. You should know better than to go there alone. The walkways are very uneven from all of the twisted roots underneath, especially near the citrus trees.' She avoided mentioning my arthritic limbs and inability to walk beyond short distances; I loved her for that sensitive avoidance of reality. But we both knew it.

'Oh, but the sunset was so beautiful last night that I could not resist a sunset stroll through the meadow to the island pond.'

As I noted the tightening of her mouth, I sympathized with my poor niece's irritation over my behavior. In truth, I would have hated it at her age, but I parted with my mother and step-father at seventeen and never had such entanglements.

I gave her hand a brief squeeze as I added, 'The gardens speak to my soul, and I cannot always resist them.' There were too many sweet memories not to indulge myself – no matter the cost. Glancing out of the back windows that overlooked the Boboli Gardens' gentle terraces, lined with cypress and oleander trees, I could almost smell the sweetly perfumed roses that grew around the Judas trees. And just beyond them stretched out a richly landscaped profusion of camellias, azaleas and hydrangeas. More aromatic sensual delights. Beyond that stood the Egyptian obelisk, surmounted by a gilded orb. It stretched skyward, straight and tall, positioned behind the Pitti Palace, the splendid residence that once housed the Medicis when they ruled Florence with their wealth and power.

I closed my eyes.

Dear God, I wish I were a girl again, moving through the gardens with a lightness of careless youth.

The Boboli Gardens were the reason that I had come back to spend my last days in these shabby rooms at the nearby Palazzo Cruciato – so I could stroll through the shaded walks of the gardens, hear the dreamy expanse of flowing fountain waters, gaze out over the whole of Florence . . . *and* remember the past.

Paula's delicate cough startled me out of my reverie. She then tapped the cover of an engraved leather book on top of the stack. 'Are you thinking about *him*? How can you?'

I winced inside.

She meant Byron. George Gordon, Lord Byron.

My lover. My enemy. My torment.

He had said to others that he had never loved me, but I knew that wasn't true. He *did* love me – in his own way. And he hurt me in every way possible.

Paula knew the details of my grand love affair, including the child who came from it. My darling daughter, Allegra. To my niece's credit, she never judged me with that pinched-faced expression of Victorian tourists who gave me a sidelong glance of pity (and curiosity) when I walked down the narrow, crooked streets of Florence. I saw them murmuring to each other behind their fans, but I pretended not to notice, smiling and nodding to each and every one of them.

Most certainly, they talked about Paula and her own illegitimate daughter, as well.

L'amore è cieco. Love is blind.

I suppose that is why my niece never judged me: we were

too similar, except in appearance. Where I had the exotic coloring of the Mediterranean climes, Paula possessed the delicate features of a pale cameo, complete with ivory complexion and soft blonde waves. An English rose to my hothouse flower.

She flipped open the thick volume and saw the inscription: *To Claire – my greatest heart's desire. B.*

'You never told me about how you met Byron.'

I smiled inwardly. 'No, I did not.'

Paula looked up, her brows raised. 'And I suppose that means that you will *not* ever tell me.'

'What has spiked this sudden interest in my past?'

'Trelawny's letter, I suppose.' She shrugged. 'He was part of your literary group, was he not?'

'Not in Geneva – he came into our lives later when we lived in Pisa, but he was certainly an . . . interesting addition with his bold, forceful presence – more Byronic than the poet himself.' I smiled.

'And he wanted to marry you?'

Trelawny. Not Byron. Not the one that I loved.

Sidestepping a direct answer with an averted glance, I continued, 'It was a long time ago, my dear – half a century – so there's no point in bringing up all of that again. I rarely think about Byron – or any of them, at all.' All lies, of course. Our little circle in Geneva during that summer of 1816 had fashioned my entire world for most of my life; they were the most precious memories of my youth and had shaped every-thing that I held sacred – even to my own detriment. My family, my friends, my lover . . . they had all often treated me with a careless affection reserved for one who was not center stage but a secondary player in their grand dramas. Still, I loved them.

1816. 'The Year Without a Summer,' as the newspapers had called it.

A volcano had exploded on the other side of world and, by June, the whole of Europe was covered by a dust cloud which made the days rainy and the nights cold with a damp chill that crept into one's very bones. Mostly, we had to take refuge inside Byron's Villa Diodati – an elegant, porticoed house perched high on the eastern shore of Lake Geneva. Even over the expanse of time, I could still hear the evening conversations around the massive stone fireplace, everyone telling ghost stories until each one of us had the germ of an idea for a poem or a book.

In truth, every day of that summer was burned in my memory and, somehow, each recollection became stronger as I grew older.

But Paula did not need to know that.

'Who would have thought you would outlive the whole lot of them?' Paula murmured, flipping through the gilt-edged pages, pausing at an illustration or two.

'Indeed – I never thought I would live this long.' They were all dead now, except for Trelawny. I would have liked for him to visit Florence before he died, but I had to content myself with his letters since travel was too arduous in the summer heat for him now.

Paula stopped on the page where I had left a bronze agate bookmark decorated with a tiny Scottish thistle on the tip. After scanning the page, she yawned. 'I never liked poetry. It always seemed so artificial to me – even Byron's work, though I know you're partial to it, of course.' She glanced at me sideways with a subtle look of amusement, but I kept my features composed and calm. Inside, I was protesting, but I would not let my niece see it. I had learned to tame my volatile temper somewhat – at least outwardly. Paula had no idea what it was like to have a great and brilliant poet express his passion for her in his work. She had never lived to hear words written about her that transcended the very language in which they were written. She had never touched the edges of fame. A heady place.

I knew exactly what poem lay on the marked page:
There be none of Beauty's daughters
With a magic like Thee . . .
Reciting the lines in my mind, I remembered when he first showed the poem to me during that haunted summer in Geneva. We had just returned to Diodati, trying to avoid a violent storm, and we dashed from his carriage though the raindrops, scrambled inside the villa with our shoes clattering on the

hard stone floor. Laughing as I shook the rain out of my hair, our eyes met in passion and longing, the cold, damp drizzle forgotten in the heat of our desire.

Afterwards, we lay in his large bed, listening to the thunder rolling down from the mountains, and he gave me a thin sheet of parchment with three stanzas of his bold handwriting scrawled across it. It had no title, but it was inscribed *To Claire from Albe*. That was our nickname for him because he regaled us so often about his adventures as a young man in Albania.

We all knew that he embellished the tales of his travels, but they kept us entertained when the incessant rain drove us indoors.

For months, I had kept the poem folded next to my heart, and I would read it again and again. It was the tangible proof of his love. Even when my feelings had later turned to hate, I could not part with the poem. It was mine, and he had been mine if only for a brief moment. He had no idea when he wrote it that I was already expecting his child.

Snapping the book shut, Paula tossed it on the stack and clicked her tongue. 'Too bad that you cannot pay bills with words on a page—'

'Perhaps you can,' I pointed out. 'At least *some* words can be turned to gold.'

'Only if you possess the type of fame of your beloved poet.' She started to exit the room.

'Or . . . if you were acquainted with a famous poet,' I posed in a sweet voice.

Paula paused, then turned slowly back in my direction. 'What are you saying? I have seen that look on your face before, and I know it means that you have some type of scheme in mind.'

'Possibly.' I slipped the letter out from under the pile of books. 'Trelawny's letter had an intriguing proposition: someone is traveling here from England and wants to see me – a man who might be interested in buying some relics from the old days . . . my letters.'

'Who wants them?' Paula's eyes kindled with excitement as she reached for the letter. I jerked it back, just out of her grasp.

'You will know – soon.'

'Stop playing games, Aunt Claire. You know we are on the edge of financial collapse. We can barely afford food from the street market, and this is the last month that we can even pay the rent on this apartment, much less any of the niceties we should be enjoying as British ladies in Italy. Do you want to see Georgiana and me *starve*?' Her voice broke toward the end of the sentence, and I refrained from rolling my eyes. Obviously, I wasn't the only one in the family with acting skills. But she was right: our time in Florence would come to an end very quickly if we did not have an influx of cash soon, and I could not allow my niece and her daughter to suffer.

'The man's name is William Michael Rossetti. I don't know him, but Trelawny has met him in London and pleads in his letter for me to receive Mr Rossetti,' I paused. 'Apparently, this man Rossetti might be interested in buying some of my Shelley correspondence . . . among other things.' *But not the poem; he cannot have the poem.* 'I suppose people have discovered that writing about famous people can be quite lucrative – the biographies of Byron and Shelley come out every year.' My eyes fell on the delicate silver inkwell that Shelley had given me; it was so pretty with a finely etched lid and filigreed base. It looked like the kind of writing tool that a poet would use, but he never actually used it. I did. Shelley liked to compose with an old wooden inkwell that he had owned when he was a student at Oxford – he said it brought the Muse to him when he needed it. And now the silver inkwell belonged to me. If I could bring myself to sell it, I would be parting with more than a memory; I would be surrendering a symbol of love and friendship.

Then again, memories did not pay the rent, and I had to make certain that Paula and Georgiana had a home.

'Write to Mr Rossetti immediately, and I will find out if he is in Florence yet,' Paula exclaimed, fetching my quill and writing paper as she muttered to herself, 'We will need to have the apartment spruced up. He cannot come here, thinking we are desperate to sell him our memorabilia at *any* price. No . . . he must see you as simply interested in sharing your memories with the world – and I as your devoted companion who wants to indulge your every whim.' She bustled around the room twice, then turned back to me, holding up the quill and paper. 'I think you must write to him today.'

I glanced up at her face, now lit with glowing eyes and a hopeful upward tilt to her lips.

It gladdened my heart, but still I hesitated, clutching Trelawny's letter in my hand. The hard reality of selling my past hit me with a wave of desolation.

Could I do it and not sell my soul?

Shaking the writing paper, Paula exhaled in a short choke of impatience. '*Please*, Aunt, write the letter – if not for me, for Georgiana.' Just then, her little girl skipped into the room, clutching her doll made of fabric scraps with a wide grin. Her fair curls bobbed as she ran in my direction and flung her arms around me in a tight embrace.

I could not resist that appeal, and Paula knew it. Her daughter, Georgiana, reminded me too much of my long-lost Allegra.

I must do it for all of us.

As I nodded, someone moved in the doorway, just out of my sight. I thought I glimpsed our man Raphael's rough cotton shirt and jet-black hair. Then I blinked, and he disappeared. Or perhaps I had imagined his hovering presence. My vision could deceive me at times . . . yet a warning voice whispered in my head to be cautious. *Be careful.*

Paula cleared her throat with deliberate intent.

Slowly, I took the quill from her with a deep, inward sigh and dipped it in the silver inkwell.

There was no going back now.

It turned out that I didn't have to wait long to receive a response from Mr Rossetti.

Paula had made inquiries at the British Consulate and found that he was already in Florence, staying at a palazzo near the Duomo – the magnificent medieval cathedral at the center of the oldest part of town. Paula was beside herself with breathless anticipation and personally gave my note to the *direttore* of his hotel; she waited for a response, which came almost instantly: Mr William Rossetti would call on us that Sunday afternoon, in two days' time.

Much cleaning, dusting and shopping ensued the next day.

Raphael said little, just quietly swept the floors. I asked him – in both English and Italian – if he had been eavesdropping yesterday, but he only shrugged with indifference. Perhaps my eyes had deceived me after all.

By late afternoon I hardly cared, so pleased we all were with our little apartment on the Via Romana; it had never looked so good, in spite of the aging furniture and cracked stone floors. Our apartment had originally been part of the Palazzo Cruciato – an elegant mansion during its heyday two hundred years ago, but now fallen on hard times since ownership had passed out of the original family. It had been subdivided into various apartments for those who enjoyed the financial state known as 'genteel poverty.'

Nevertheless, Paula had even bought fresh flowers – yellow roses – to adorn the tea table in my room. It was decided (because of my sprained ankle) that I would receive Mr Rossetti there, seated decorously on the bed, wearing my best gray striped silk dress (no stains or frayed hems) and lace cap. If we had planned to perform the scene on stage, it couldn't have been more rehearsed. We even practiced our conversation until it sounded like dialog from the Teatro. By bedtime, though, fatigue had set in and my ankle throbbed.

But Paula still blazed with energy – and endless warnings.

Don't scare him away, Aunt.

I promise not to.

Don't agree to any sale of letters until I have reviewed the amount.

I promise not to.

Don't talk too much.

I cannot promise that one.

I have to confess that I, too, felt the thrill of having a British visitor in the apartment, even if he wanted nothing more than to buy relics from my past. Silly that one never completely moves past the tug of the mother country.

And so, on the afternoon of June 14, 1873, at two p.m., Mr William Michael Rossetti appeared at our door.

As planned, Paula greeted him and then brought our guest

to my large bedroom where a pot of tea and two cups awaited on my writing desk, and the windows were thrown open to catch the late-day breeze. A soft scent of jasmine wafted through the room, and I could hear the cathedral bells in the distance ringing across the city on the hour. If I had not been in my semi-dotage, receiving a man young enough to be my son would have been almost delicious. *Almost.* Unfortunately, old age ruled out any thoughts of that for me.

Beauty's daughter had faded.

'Miss Clairmont?'

I glanced at the slim gentleman at the threshold of my room, dressed discreetly in a suit of black, with a white shirt and neatly tied cravat. He had a receding hairline and an angular face, but kind eyes. 'May I enter?'

Paula hovered behind him, flashing an anxious look in my direction. 'Of course you can – my aunt has been looking forward to meeting you,' she responded for me. 'I shall collect you again, Mr Rossetti, after teatime.'

He gave a small bow to my niece.

Once Paula had vanished from the room, I gestured for him to take a seat in the flowered wingback chair near the window and commented, 'The heat of Florence must seem quite oppressive compared with England – we are having an especially warm June.' Of course, I opened our tête-à-tête with the weather – another tug from the mother country.

'I find the Italian summer quite a refreshing change from the so-called sunny season of London, Miss Clairmont.' Smiling, he inched the chair closer to me and sat down. 'And I might add that Florence is especially to my liking in other ways. The city of great painters and sculptors – Giotto, Michelangelo, Botticelli . . . what could be more delightful? My brother is an artist, so I am viewing all of the beauties of the city for both of us.'

'How lovely for you – and him.' I rearranged the folds of my dress to cover the swollen ankle. 'I apologize for not standing to greet you.'

'It seems most wise, considering your injury.' His pleasant features kindled with polite concern. Paula must have told him about the sprained ankle – perhaps for sympathy? I would accept those sentiments, of course. *Desperate times required desperate measures.*

'It has been . . . uncomfortable,' I admitted.

'As such, I am most grateful that you agreed to see me . . .' Mr Rossetti's words trailed off as he adjusted the lapels of his jacket.

'Actually, I was most happy to meet you after my old friend Edward Trelawny made a case very strongly that I should receive you.' I lounged back against the soft pillows. 'How can I be of help, Mr Rossetti?'

He gave a short laugh. 'Your directness is most refreshing . . . As you might know from Trelawny, I have obtained some unpublished materials written by Percy Bysshe Shelley, who was married to your sister—'

'He was married to my *stepsister*, Mary – she and I were not related by blood, though her father, Godwin, wed my mother.' I corrected him with an inward sigh; I had no *real* father. 'Certainly, I did consider Shelley my brother-in-law after their marriage – and, even more so, I considered him my dearest friend.' *Much to Mary's dismay*, I added silently. She had always thought we were too close, and I knew the rumors that had circulated about us over the years: I had been accused of being Shelley's lover, the mother of his illicit child and so forth. Totally false and a discredit to his memory, but people loved to gossip about us.

'I misspoke,' he added hastily. 'I was aware of the family connections, though many probably assume since you and Mary were raised together, that she was—'

'My sister? A common misconception.' I involuntarily stiffened, remembering my precarious position in the Shelley household. 'Indeed, we were always very affectionate in our dealings and, later, correspondence. I lived with her and Shelley for most of their married life – we were quite content in each other's company.' *Most of the time.* 'Of course, once Shelley died and Mary moved back to England with their child, we stayed in contact mostly through letters until her death.' A pang of sadness rang out inside of me. A deep vein of loss. No one felt Mary's demise more keenly than I – not even her son, who did not invite me to the funeral.

Mr Rossetti shifted in his chair, obviously discomfited by the turn of our conversation. 'The world mourned the loss of *Frankenstein*'s author. Her like will never be seen again – and that goes without a doubt for Shelley, as well.'

'Yes, they belong to the ages now,' I mused, keeping my emotions under control by staring at the ceiling fresco of sweet-faced cherubs floating on fluffy white clouds in paradise. 'Fame has a way of elevating even the most ordinary person into a rarified world of angelic perfection, but it's a far cry from the chaos of real life.'

'You speak from experience, I imagine.' He stroked his beard, watching me quizzically as if I were a puzzle he had not quite figured out.

'More from the perspective of looking back over a long life.' Taking in a deep breath, I exhaled slowly, realizing that I had moved off the script. How much could I actually tell this man about the now-revered literary friends of my youth who complained about cold food at the breakfast table, who were short-tempered with the servants and careless about other people's feelings? 'I knew Byron and Shelley at their greatest – and lowest – moments; I suppose now the world sees them through the lens of their poetry, but I knew them as men . . . and very human ones at that. I believe Byron himself said he could not be his own hero while shaving.'

'Indeed.' Mr Rossetti settled deeper into the chair and crossed his legs. His trousers bore a neat fold at the ankles, leading to shoes that had been polished to a high shine. 'I cannot imagine anything *less* heroic.'

My mouth curved into a smile, which he echoed.

Adjusting the pillow behind my head, I finally relaxed in his presence. 'So back to the unpublished materials . . . I assume that you are interested in purchasing more?' There. I had said it.

He nodded vigorously. 'Our mutual friend, Trelawny, said that you might be interested in . . . parting with some of the correspondence that occurred between you and members of the Byron/Shelley circle. You may or may not know that Mary and her sole remaining son, Percy, wrote a biography of her husband years ago, and it set off a flurry of works about the poet ever since. It seems that everyone wants to know about Shelley – and Byron, of course – and there is no part of his life too insignificant for our audience today.'

'But not too shocking?' I raised my brows. 'I may be living some distance away from England, but I have read Mary's biography of Shelley and I found it very . . . suitable for Victorian sensibilities.' Actually, I hadn't read it, but Paula told me that it seemed to have glossed over some of the more scandalous parts of our history, and minimized *my* role in their lives considerably.

'So you did not find it entirely truthful?' he posed.

'Is anything, especially when it comes to family?'

A long pause stretched between us like a tense band, with both of us trying to find our way beyond the social niceties to the core of honesty in each other's character. I could not part with my letters to anyone who was not worthy of preserving the truth.

The ormolu clock on the mantle ticked away: a steady beat of two mechanical lovebirds that mirrored each step of time one from the other – moment to moment.

The silence stretched on.

I glanced at his neatly pressed trousers and shiny shoes once again. Would a deceitful character have taken such pains with his attire? Still . . . I hesitated.

'How well I know about those family "complications," since we are a family of Italian immigrant eccentrics,' he mused quietly. 'My brother, Dante Gabriel, is the erratic painter destined to be famous, and my sister, Christina, is the serious, obsessive poet who cannot help but be the genius she was born to be. That leaves me – a writer of no great talent, and an artist of even less skill. Maybe it's our destiny to simply be the glass through which history views their greatness.'

My eyes met his and nothing but gentle understanding glowed from the depths. 'It seems as if we both have had the privilege and misfortune of being "attached" to the famous,' I murmured, half to myself.

'Did you say "shackled"?'

'Touché.'

'So will you consider selling your correspondence to me?

I would like to write my own biography of Shelley, and having your letters would fill in many of the gaps from the Geneva and Pisa years that recent biographers have perhaps distorted . . .'

Rubbing my ankle, I suddenly began to find this whole conversation exhausting. 'I expect they would. But I'm not sure that I can help you . . . or that it would be a good thing after all to contradict everyone's elevated recollections of Shelley. If the world wants to see him like that, who am I to burst that fantasy? I was only a minor player in their drama—'

'You are not even that,' he said.

Blinking in momentary confusion, I forgot all about my ankle. 'What do you mean?'

'In the latest revision of Shelley's biography by his son and his wife, at Mary's behest apparently, you are not even mentioned by name – just a one-sentence reference as "Mary's stepsister."' He cleared his throat. 'I apologize for blurting it out, but you just said you had read the biography, and I assumed you preferred . . . the anonymity.'

'You assumed incorrectly, sir.' Shock hit me – hard and strong – as if I had been slapped in the face by my own family. I had been wronged. 'But it was *I* who cared for Mary and Shelley's son when he was a child. How could he? And Mary's betrayal cuts to my heart. When she almost died from a miscarriage in La Spezia, it was I who held her in a bath of ice to stop the bleeding. I saved her life . . .' My words ended on a note of outrage.

If I had been relegated to a mere side note, no doubt my daughter, Allegra, had been deleted completely from our history.

Tears stung my eyes, and I blinked them back. 'I must apologize, Mr Rossetti, but I find myself growing quite fatigued. If you would like to stay and share a refreshment with my niece, Paula, I certainly don't mind, but I need to rest.' All pleasant words and good manners – yet, inside, I felt as if I were fading miles and miles away from the bedroom into a dream world between the past and the present where no firm, steady reality was to be found. Lies, all lies. They lied by omission.

'I'm sorry to have upset you, Miss Clairmont, with my lack of sensitivity. It was certainly not my intention. In fact, I believe the Shelley family—'

'If you please, I must insist that you leave.' My voice was firm, final. I could not bear to hear another word today.

Maybe not ever.

He rose to his feet and gave a small bow. 'Perhaps we could continue our conversation at a later time?'

I did not respond, just motioned for him to leave – which he did, eventually, after pouring me a cup of tea and pleading with me to hear him out regarding one last point.

No. I would not listen to another word.

My shock had turned to anger: pure rage at the 'sister' who could never accept that her husband found me a companion when he was at his darkest moments. The sister who found her steps dogged by bleak periods of depression and longed to have my buoyant outlook on life. The sister who craved to give birth to a daughter like my little Allegra. And she had passed that envy on to her son, so he could expunge me from their lives for all time and the world would know less and less of my role.

It would be as if I never had existed – or I had never borne a daughter.

Swiping the tears away, I reached for the teacup Mr Rossetti had set next to my bed, but my hands shook so badly that some of the dark liquid spilled on my satin coverlet. I grasped the rim of the cup with my other hand to steady it as I downed the pungent tea; it trickled down my throat and spread through my body in a soothing wave. In a few minutes, I felt my heartbeat quieten somewhat, though my right hand still had a small tremor as I clasped the empty cup.

How dare she? How dare any of them? They had tried to purge me from the past as if I were a piece of forgotten furniture to be discarded. Perhaps Trelawny was even in on the conspiracy and had contacted Mr Rossetti to buy my Shelley correspondence so he could destroy it. Then there would be even less of me that would survive.

I would *not* let that happen.

Setting the teacup back on the saucer, it caught the edge

and both pieces tipped to the floor, splashing the cup's contents on to the rug. As I watched the stain spread, I dropped my head in my hands, finally giving in to the tears – weeping with a deep sense of lost dreams and endless trials. What was the use of fighting for a place in history when everyone was determined to erase my very existence?

Maybe invisibility was my destiny.

I eased off the bed to retrieve the broken china and blot up the tea splotch. Then I noticed a small, folded note of marbleized paper lying next to the saucer. It must have been under the cup and fallen out when the china tipped on to the floor.

Reaching down, I picked up the note and slowly unfolded it and scanned the lone sentence scrawled on the paper.

I gasped as I read the words: *Your daughter lives.*

My hand went to the silver cross pendant at my chest, covering it with my fingers as I read the words over and over again.

What did it mean? Allegra had died long ago when she was but five years old.

Had Mr Rossetti placed the note there? Why?

Heart pounding, I felt as if my world had begun to tilt off its axis, altering my beliefs about the past and the people I loved. Hearing about Mary's heartless treachery was bad enough, but now someone was stirring up the ghost of hope about my long-departed daughter, Allegra.

Am I going mad?

I started to call out for Paula, but I paused. She and Georgiana were vulnerable, and if Mr Rossetti had come here to trick or swindle us, they could be placed in the path of an unscrupulous man.

Was he an ally or an enemy? I did not know.

Surely it was not a coincidence that the note appeared the day of his visit.

Looking at the words once more, I searched my mind for a fragment of memory that would make it true, but I could summon no such recollections.

Unless Shelley and Mary lied about Allegra's fate when they told me she died of typhus at the convent school in Bagnacavallo.

Was that possible? I could scarcely entertain the notion.

I thought I knew the truth of what happened all those years ago, but perhaps they had all conspired against me. Closing my eyes, I felt the present slip away into the past. The summer of dreams and passion. Love and light. And that wretched volcano, Tambora. When it erupted, it set a chain of events into motion that stretched beyond its physical boundaries into a timeless reality.

It turned the world to fire and ash.

Captain Parker's Log
April 5, 1815
Makassar (240 miles north-east of Mount Tambora)

When I heard the loud boom, I thought it was cannon fire – a blast of sound that awakened me from my deep-sea slumber. Heart pounding, I rose from my bunk just at the moment that I heard another thunderous crack and then another, so many that my ship, the Fortuna, *shuddered in the water. Dear God . . . pirates had found us and were attacking. Fear flooded through me as I pulled on my breeches, grabbed a pistol and raced up the stairs.*

We had been docked at Makassar, on the southwest coast on the Sulawesi Island, for a fortnight, ready to set sail for England with our rich cargo of exotic spices, teas, and oils; but corsairs had been sighted throughout the Indian Ocean and I decided to delay our departure. Perhaps that had been a mistake. As I took the steps two at a time, my breath coming in gasps, I realized that we may have stayed too long.

More blasts echoed through the night air as I arrived on deck, my crew scrambling to the rails to scan the waters, anxiously murmuring among themselves.

'Stay calm, men,' I ordered in a firm voice. 'We are a sturdy ship and can meet any challenges.' In truth, the Fortuna *was a forty-foot merchant vessel with a crew of fewer than eighty men, all of whom were sailors, not soldiers. We were most vulnerable to pirates, especially*

since our cruiser carried a storage of silks, teas and opium for the British East India Company. A rich prize.

If they began to fire their cannons at us, we would be easily taken, for we carried no artillery and few weapons. Our best strategy would be to head out to sea and try to outrun any rogue pirates.

The ship rocked violently with the next blast, and a few of my men shouted in fear.

'Courage! We will protect our ship at all costs,' I exclaimed. I would never allow pirates to take my cargo. This was my chance to achieve wealth and fame, which was denied me as a younger son of an upper-class English family. I had spent two years in this godforsaken part of the world to earn my fortune, and I would not give up even one jar of precious oil. Never.

Just then, the booms ceased, the Fortuna *stilled and the air turned eerily quiet.*

Taking advantage of the moment, I raced to the bow and scanned the waters off to the north, squinting in the moonless, black night, trying to catch sight of a pirate ship. But I saw nothing. I heard only the quiet lap of waves against the hull of my ship, steady and rhythmic.

Then I glanced at the smaller vessels docked nearby. They showed no sign of activity, most likely because their crews were on shore leave.

The men joined me one by one, but we said nothing more.

Damp, humid air seemed to grow even heavier as I waited and watched with my crew. Clutching the pistol, I struggled to keep my dread at bay as the minutes passed slowly, and still we heard no more cannon fire.

'Maybe it was thunder,' one of my crew whispered in an anxious voice.

I was not convinced.

Gazing upward, I searched in vain for a break in the clouds to allow the moon an instant to beam its light upon us. Instead, I felt a droplet against my face. Then another . . . and another. The soft sprinkle of rainfall had begun. Perhaps it had been thunder after all, heralding a tropical storm.

Blinking rapidly, I felt the drizzle grow stronger, coming down in heavy waves. But it felt oddly dry and powdery and tasted like grains of sand dropping from the sky. It was not a storm. It was not rain.

It was volcanic ash.

Without conscious intention, I began to pray. Pray to God. Pray to Fate. Pray for redemption of my sins.

Was this the end of the world?

TWO

Geneva, Switzerland, May 1816

'Byron is going to be here *soon* – I can feel it,' I exclaimed, my eyes darting back and forth between Mary and Shelley. She had a piece of needlework in her hand, as always – some bit of white muslin with embroidered flowers on it – but I couldn't sit long enough to hold a needle, much less sew with it. Shelley had his favorite volume of some Greek playwright in hand. He looked up; she did not.

'I heard his cortege made a procession from the coast of France almost as if he were royalty: several carts, animals, servants – and his own carriage, which is a replica of the one that Napoleon traveled in,' Shelley commented, an ironic twist to his mouth. 'I think he may find us distressingly simple.'

'More like impoverished,' Mary murmured as she leaned over and adjusted the blanket that covered her infant son, William, in his hand-carved wooden cradle. He slept during this delicate maneuver, never uttering a peep, even as Mary stroked his cheek. The temperatures were unseasonably cool for summer, and she was quite nervous over the state of William's health.

'I will *not* let either of you dampen my enthusiasm for seeing Byron again. I have longed for him to be here with us. It seems as if a lifetime has passed since I last saw him, even though it has only been a few months.' Glancing around the modest little sitting area of our rooms at the Hotel d'Angleterre, I felt a pang of uncertainty that he would ever show up.

Byron was the one who had wanted to meet in Geneva, and had become all the more eager when he knew I traveled with Shelley – a poet almost as notorious as he. His letters, while hardly passionate (could I blame him with his life in shambles?), had been encouraging that we would be together again. But he made no mention as to his arrival date, even when I playfully accused him of being an old man for all the lack of speed he had displayed in arriving in Geneva. Surely he would be happy to see me again?

Yes, he would. I knew it in my heart and soul. I was *not* just a passing fancy.

Shelley and Mary exchanged a cautious glance, and it caused a flare of irritation inside of me. Who were *they* to judge and be cautious? A married man and his mistress? Even though Mary traveled as 'Mrs Shelley,' his wife, Harriet, still lived and resided in England with their two children. Could anything be more hypocritical than to disapprove of my actions? Mary had her great poet – why should I not have mine?

I had even introduced Mary to Byron in London, and she remarked repeatedly afterwards that he was so 'mild and mannerly.' So why was she now urging me to be more temperate in my feelings?

Byron had left England a week before we did; he should have reached us already, even if he had altered his travel plans en route and chosen another hotel.

No, that could not be. Every traveling British tourist stayed at the Hotel d'Angleterre since it was a stop on the Grand Tour for people with the money to journey in style. The best hostelry in Geneva, it was located in the suburb of Sécheron, at the southernmost tip of the lake, just outside the walls of the city to avoid the ten o'clock curfew when the gates closed on all evening soirees. Luxury and revelry. Byron would not be able to resist stopping here.

Perhaps it was not wise that I had been haunting the hotel's lobby for a sight of him, but I could not restrain myself. When he did arrive, he would no doubt be given luxury quarters with a private entrance, so I had to keep my watch for the moment he appeared; otherwise, it could be days before we actually met again.

How unfortunate that all we could afford was this cheap set of rooms on the upper floor, far from the grand entrance. Needless to say, aside from the view of the lake and streets below, our quarters had modest appointments – tiny spaces and bare floors, along with outdated wallpaper with its scenes of the Napoleonic Wars. Hardly the type of residence for Shelley;

after all, he *was* the son of an earl. But then again, the three of us were living in a type of limbo – not servants yet not respectable. Our families had disowned us and the creditors had hounded us out of London, but we somehow managed to survive.

Still, who could not be happy when pursuing love to its natural end, even if the whole world shunned us?

'Where *is* he?' With dragging steps, I moved to the window, almost willing him to appear below. But only a young boy ambled along the rainy street, his shoes slipping on the wet, uneven cobblestones. He snatched a rose from the flower cart, and an old woman clad in black yelled after him, shaking her hand as she spat on the ground. As the rain began to fall in heavy sheets, she pushed the cart slowly down the street, leaving only gray emptiness.

I sighed and turned away from the window.

'When is this incessant rain going to stop?' Mary moaned as she focused once more on her needlework and rubbed her forehead. She probably had a headache again; she had had one every couple of days since the baby's birth. 'I don't think we have had one clear day—'

'It's all the fault of that volcano – Mount Tambora,' Shelley said, setting one book on the floor next to his chair and picking up another that had been tucked in the side of his chair cushion. 'I read it in the paper today. A volcano erupted on the other side of the world late last year; it consumed whole villages in liquid fire and blasted a cloud of thick and dusky ashes into the sky. Just imagine the power of that explosion.'

Intrigued, I drew closer to them. 'How does that affect us?'

'The ash cloud will be drifting over Europe for the next few months, and it is so large that the sun will hardly be able to penetrate it.' Shelley paused for dramatic effect. 'I think the rain and cold are likely to be with us for the entire summer – a fitting veil between us and the divine light of the heavens.'

'Surely not.' Mary's delicate features drew together in a frown. 'That is terribly depressing.'

'Stop trying to frighten us, Shelley. Who cares about the gray skies?' I shrugged, rising from the widow seat. 'It rains most of the time in England, so we are used to it. Every day is dreary in London. At least here we have the possibility of sunshine.'

'Ever the optimist, Claire,' my sister commented with a twist to her lips that could never have been taken for a smile.

'No, she is simply a woman in love,' Shelley chimed in, reaching for my hand. I clasped his slender fingers briefly, the skin smooth and soft as befitting a lord's son who had never done a day's worth of manual labor. Mary noted my gesture and frowned.

She had no reason to be jealous, but I could tell that she found my presence intrusive at times. An interloper in their relationship.

'Claire has found her poet, her inspiration – the man who will spend his days writing verse to her fine, dark eyes.' Shelley made a gesture of appeal toward Mary. 'We want her to have what we share together, do we not, my love?'

She smiled, her forehead tranquil once more. 'Of course.'

I leaned down and hugged her, stroking her fine hair. 'I may never have a connection as powerful as yours, but I shall never tire of looking for it.'

Mary submitted to my embrace but turned her head away from me – she had eyes only for Shelley.

I watched the two of them exchange another glance – this time of deep rapture – and I felt a twinge of uncertainty again at my own attachment. Unlike Mary and Shelley, my love and I had not found an instantaneous connection of heart and mind – the type of passion that made everything in life pale by comparison. In truth, I had pursued Byron shamelessly in London. I admit it. Knowing that he was at the Drury Lane Theater, I had arranged for an audition with him on the pretext that I wanted to become an actress. I didn't really want to act on the stage, though; I wanted to be *his* leading lady, and I made certain that he noticed me. He protested that our age gap was too great: he had turned twenty-eight and I was but seventeen. But I would not be deterred. I showed him some of my poetry, then I sang for him and he was captivated; he said my voice could make the angels weep.

I don't know that it was true love, but after we made love, I knew he would be mine. *Forever.*

Glancing at the mirror across the room, I checked my reflection with a saucy tilt of my head: dark curls, deep brown eyes and smooth olive skin from my unknown father. Almost Italian. Nothing like Mary with her pale, refined features and serious expression. But I had an eager animation that I knew how to work to my advantage, even if I was not a great beauty like my stepsister.

Byron said I possessed the fire and ice of a Mediterranean temperament, not quite tamed by a British upbringing. Perhaps it was true. My father may have been one of the rebels that he wrote about in his poetry and my mother was certainly English and tried every way she could to make me rein in my emotions. Alas, to no avail.

'Perhaps we should go to the quay to hire a boat for the evening. If Byron arrives, he will already be on the lake,' I suggested as I drifted around the room, my fingers trailing the furniture edges. He had told me about his celebrated swim of Hellespont when he was a young man in Greece, recounting how he felt the equal of any man when mastering a powerful wave with stroke after stroke, his clubfoot out of sight. It also soothed his fiery imagination to be near an expanse of water, either swimming or boating.

Mary opened her mouth, and I knew she would urge caution, but Shelley cut in quickly as he took a quick glance out the window, 'I see nothing wrong with strolling to the lake and hiring a boat – if the rain lets up. Perhaps we shall make our way to Yvoire this time to see the medieval castle, and if we happen to catch a glimpse of the great man himself, well, then, would that not be a prize indeed?'

'Yes, we *must* go to Yvoire,' I pronounced. 'I shall get our capes, Mary. A walk will be good for William and you, for we must provide him with fresh air for his lungs and you with exercise for your frail limbs. We have been shut up here for much too long.' Smiling, I exited the room to retrieve our walking gear.

Today would be my reunion with Byron. *I knew it.*

An hour later the sky had cleared. Happily, we made our way through the elegant lobby graced with marble floors and

Grecian pillars, then ambled toward the shoreline with its row of small boats awaiting tourists who desired to explore the beauty and delights of Lake Geneva. Early on in our stay, we had sailed our way from village to village, most of them isolated and rural, and gloried in the swath of colors that stretched across the mountains to the east at sunrise, with Mont Blanc looming in the distance.

The lake felt almost like a presence as it watched us and we watched it in endless fascination. Always changing. A chameleon of color and texture depending on the weather and time of day. At times, it stretched out with a startling, sky-blue color when lit by the sun's glow, then it would turn a murky, cobalt shade as the storms rolled in. As our little sailboat crisscrossed the lake, I would trail my fingers in the water; it always felt cool, even on the hottest day.

But now our trips were becoming less frequent as the showers would often be accompanied by startling thunderstorms – strong and violent – churning up the waves into swelling whitecaps.

Our familiar boatman approached immediately as we reached the quay. '*Mesdames, Monsieur, comment puis-je vous aider?*'

'*S'il vous plait, nous avons besoin de louerun bateau pour aller à Yvoire,*' I responded, being the only member of our little group who spoke French well enough to ask to hire a boat to take us to the medieval town on the east shore.

The boatman gestured toward a small wooden vessel with a tall mast and two sails, and Shelley nodded. He loved boats, in spite of the fact that he could not swim. He loved drifting along the lake for hours, trying to the master the intricacies of catching the wind.

Just then, his face took on a glow of awe as he gazed out at the jagged mountain peaks off in the distance, capped with snow. 'Can the world contain such beauty?'

My breath caught in my throat. *No, it could not.*

But I wasn't looking at the Alps; I had spied my beloved poet as he stepped out of a rowboat. Dressed in a black coat and black pants strapped around his boots, he moved across the dock with that peculiar gliding gait from his clubfoot, which only added to his mystique. A hush descended on passers-by as their faces turned to catch a glimpse of his Grecian features, which were almost too beautiful for a man.

As if sensing my presence, he turned and our eyes locked.

I gasped at what I saw in the depths of his sad, tortured gaze. He had changed since I last saw him. Older, with faint lines stretched across his forehead. Some gray hair threaded through his curls even though he was not yet thirty. I could only think that the scandal of his failed marriage had aged him well beyond his years. He seemed lost.

And he was *not* happy to see me.

My heart sank under the weight of the despair that assailed me.

What would I do if he simply walked away?

Then his glance moved to Shelley, and he brightened as if a candle had been lit inside of him. He slowly, haltingly moved in our direction, and I ushered Mary and Shelley forward as I murmured under my breath to her, 'You *must* be friends – for my sake.' Mary gasped and hesitated, but Shelley eagerly closed the distance between them, making his bow with all the elegance of his aristocratic heritage – something not lost on Byron.

Quickly, I did the introductions and let the men indulge in easy small talk that seemed to bode well for a friendship to ripen. And why should they not find mutual connection? They were both handsome and brilliant . . . and social outcasts from the aristocratic society to which they had been born.

Relief flooded through me.

I might have a chance after all at the life I longed for as the inspiration for a great man.

Mary cleared her throat with deliberate impatience, and Shelley immediately brought her forward. 'Forgive me for being so remiss in reacquainting you with my soul's twin: Mary Godwin. I believe that you met her last in London.'

'Yes, indeed.' He turned toward us, all charm and smiles.

'It is a pleasure, my lord.' She held out her hand and Byron bent over it, not quite letting his lips touch her fingers. It was very old fashioned but strangely fitting in this time and place. Obviously enchanted, Mary instantly dropped the air of reserve that surrounded her like a protective shield.

'What luck that we are all here,' Byron said, his eyes now

warm and affectionate as they rested on me again. 'I could not imagine a more congenial group in all of Geneva—'

'Nor I,' I cut in quickly. Too quickly.

I heard a man clear his throat. He stood behind Byron – younger and taller and leaner, but with the same poetic look: open collar and hair carefully arranged in artful disarray; his eyes were darker, though, full of secrets and hidden intentions. I shivered.

Byron turned and flicked his hand carelessly. 'This is my personal physician, Doctor John Polidori – he joined me before I left England, since my recent "troubles" have caused fits of nervous agitation. Quite painful really with their intensity and duration. But you look after me so carefully, do you not, John?'

'I try, my lord.' He scanned us with a wary detachment as though we were experiments in his lab – creatures to be monitored and analyzed. 'Though I cannot always protect you from that which would cause the most harm.' His glance fastened on me with a hard glare.

Not exactly sure why, I realized in that moment that Polidori would be my enemy – or, at the very least, not a friend.

'My young companion here also has a desire to write a novel – imagine that? A doctor and an author?' Byron turned back to us, ignoring the brief frown that Polidori shot at him. 'Do you think it is possible for a man of medicine also to be lit with the creative spark? I find it difficult to reconcile the two aspects of human nature.'

'Let us remember the magnificent Hippocrates who was not only a physician but also a great writer—' Shelley began.

'Of medical texts,' Byron chimed in.

'The *Hippocratic Corpus* is pure poetry, some would say.' Shelley was undaunted in his response, and Byron seemed delighted to be challenged in such a manner.

Polidori mumbled something that was incomprehensible and then spun on his heel, heading back to the rowboat. In one smooth movement, he untied the rope and jumped into the vessel, taking up the oars in both hands.

Shelley shouted for him to return, but he pulled away quickly and headed across the lake.

Byron laughed. 'Don't concern yourself with Polidori. He

is quite highly strung and will be back by dinnertime, chattering your ears off. Having traveled with him from England, through France, I can tell you he is both a tortured soul and an absurd abstraction.'

'A bit harsh.' Shelley's features puckered with distress. 'I always think it benefits us to err on the side of compassion, not criticism. Aristotle would have us believe that modesty and reason will always steer us in the direction of goodness—'

'I can see, my dear Shelley, we shall have much to discuss should I remain in Geneva. And I now think that I must stay here, if only to talk poetry and politics with you.'

Shelley bowed. 'I warn you, though, the women will not allow us to monopolize the conversation. No one is more fixed in her opinions than Mary – unless it is Claire.'

I heard Mary give a little murmur of gratitude.

'I expect no less from Godwin and Mary Wollstonecraft's daughter,' Byron continued, looking from her to me. 'Or Godwin's stepdaughter.'

My cheeks flushed at the compliment. 'We should *all* find residences here – away from the hotel – so we can enjoy each other's . . . company,' I proposed before I could stop myself. 'I cannot imagine a more pleasant way to spend the summer.'

All eyes became riveted on me. Mary pinched my arm, as if to warn me not to reveal myself so blatantly. I could not help it. What was the point in hiding how I felt?

'My sister presumes too much,' Mary said, her voice taking on the long-suffering tone of familial exasperation.

'Nonsense,' Byron pronounced. 'This is as good a place as any other to create a circle of cordiality with expatriates. I've sorely missed it.'

As he and Shelley chattered away as if long-lost acquaintances, my spirits soared ever higher.

What luck, indeed.

That afternoon, the rain continued steadily, with thick, gray clouds hovering overhead in unrelenting gloom, but nothing could dampen our enthusiasm. We practically floated back to our rooms, after having made a promise to join Byron and Polidori for supper in a private room at the hotel the next evening. He wanted to dine with his physician and Shelley tonight in an exclusive male-only gathering. I didn't care where we all came together again, as long as I would have the chance to resume the relationship of my heart's desire. Still, I barely slept after Shelley left to join him, wondering if the poets would find shared interests.

The next morning, our little trio convened early for breakfast in our sitting room, Mary and I consumed with curiosity while little William dozed peacefully in his cradle.

Shelley's good-humored smile told me everything that I needed to know about their conversation last night, and I could finally relax in the knowledge that the two men had found common ground.

Then, as he related the details of their congenial gathering the previous evening, my spirits soared.

'I don't believe any of the rumors about him,' Mary commented as she set out the delicate china for tea, lovingly handling the teapot that had belonged to her mother – one of the few items she had packed for her elopement. Fitting, since her bold adventure bore the stamp of her parents' behavior when they had first met and become lovers. 'Byron is as fine a gentleman as I have ever met – quite amiable, really.'

'I agree.' Shelley had already resumed his position in his chair, book in hand. 'We found we had much in common – our politics are quite similar, though our poetic tastes diverge. He has quite a distressing affinity for the Roman poets, not Greek.'

Seating myself next to Mary, I carefully scooped out the precious exotic tea from a small wooden caddy we had brought with us. Unbeknownst to my mother, I had nipped some of her favorite black oolong tea before we left London – just enough for a few more months if we were frugal in our portions. 'You are both English gentlemen, though Byron went to Cambridge and you attended Oxford. A connection in birth and upbringing,' I pointed out.

'Guilty as charged – not that I believe in any of that rubbish,' he added, absently flipping the pages of his book. 'One day, we will live in a classless society where all men are judged on merit alone, not ancestry or connections.'

'And women, as well, I trust,' Mary spoke up.

'Indeed, yes, my love,' Shelley enthused. 'We would not honor the memory of your great mother if we did not acknowledge the superior minds of your sex—'

'I agree: women are superior to men in every way.' I waved my hand with a flourish. 'Why is it women cannot work as men do, making their own way in the world? I want to travel and take in all of life, whether it seems becoming to do so as a woman or not – just as Mary's mother did. She was in France during the great Revolution and she roamed Europe as a gypsy, taking lovers and bearing her children on her own terms.' I felt a kindling passion inside of me as I remembered the early days of my meetings with Byron. *I* had been the sexual aggressor in our relationship – not that he was unreceptive, by any means. But I saw no reason not to arrange matters so we could have private meetings and explore all manner of physical expression of that love.

Why should I not have pursued my desires just because I was a woman?

I shared none of this information with Mary, though, since I suspected that she might not approve. I had learned to hold my tongue on such matters with my stepsister. It seemed odd that she could be quite conservative in her social views of the behavior of others, but I had already learned that people often disapproved of the very thing they themselves did regularly. Byron called it 'cant' and railed against it; I called it 'human nature' and accepted it.

'Why, Claire, you sound like a revolutionary yourself. Next, you will be penning your *own* version of the rights of women.' Shelley cheered me on, then continued, 'And I do agree with you on several counts: all men and women should be free to love at will. Marriage is a restriction of the heart and mind – a trap that binds people legally, sometimes long after the affection has disappeared.'

Mary turned paler, if such a thing were possible. As she poured the tea into chipped china cups, her hand trembled. 'I know you mean dear Harriet – and I can honestly say that I feel nothing but guilt when I meditate on the pain that I must have caused her.'

'Do not distress yourself, my dear. I still have high hopes

that she will decide to join us at some point and live with us as a sister, so we can all share in the joys of true and deep connection.'

Everyone in the group fell silent. *Harriet.* Shelley's wife. Sweet and delicate, she was the ghost in the room, always between Mary and Shelley, even though he had invited her to join us and live with him as brother and sister. He was amazed that she did not take him up on the offer, so they could all reside together as one happy family.

Mary was baffled at his suggestion, but I was amused.

As much as Shelley knew about poetry and philosophy, he seemed quite naive about the workings of the human heart. For a woman like Harriet – of a more advanced age (by scarcely five years) and lower class – to be supplanted by a brilliant beauty like Mary was the greatest insult of all, and not one she would like to be reminded of on a daily basis. Even worse, when the object of one's love is no longer interested in the pleasures of her body, it had to cut deeper than the stab of a blade.

And then there were Harriet and Shelley's children. Who would be their mother in this proposed *ménage à trois*?

'If Harriet agreed to this scheme, would you then divorce her?' Mary asked in a quiet voice. *And wed me?* She did not speak the words, but I knew she was thinking them.

At this point in our lives, Mary (and I) had no male protector except Shelley; without the embrace of father or husband, we were adrift in a world that was still controlled by men. And society did not look kindly on women who eloped with married men or supported causes that were perceived as 'unfeminine.'

In short, Mary and I were ruined, and we both knew it. William's birth had added another element: what would be his status with his father still married to another woman? Quite the tangled web.

Shelley's features grew somber, and I realized that he had never really considered the details of his 'proposal' that we all live together as one loving family. I almost laughed. It was a quality of his that was so endearing, yet maddening. Truly, the idealist lives in a world that has little to do with us mere mortals, and Shelley was a man of lofty principles inside and out. From his constant philosophizing on his beloved Greek poets to his strict vegetarian diet, he lived what he preached, almost to a fault. That was the maddening part: he didn't understand how these practices could harm those around him.

But who was I to question following one's passion? I had ruined myself with England's most notorious poet and gloried in every moment of my fall.

Mary sniffed. She expected an answer from him.

Still he seemed reluctant. 'Yes, I would divorce Harriet and ask you to be my wife,' he finally said with a tender light in his eyes. 'Even though such formalities insult the true and profound nature of our feelings, I want to make you happy in all ways.'

Mary exhaled in relief – just a tiny sigh, but I heard it. She longed for some degree of respectability in her relationship with Shelley, but she would never have it in the way she longed for, even if Harriet divorced Shelley and they were able to wed. Mary would always be known as the 'other woman' – now and in the future. Her own brand of idealism often expected the best of people, whereas I expected the worst, but it didn't bother me. Perhaps, again, it stemmed from the lack of a father; I knew how cruel public opinion could be for those individuals who did not follow conventions. It took the wings of an angel to fly above the fray of criticism. Shelley had those wings, but Mary did not.

I sipped my tea, glancing from one to the other – Shelley had resumed reading *Antigone*, one of his favorite plays, and Mary preoccupied herself with fitting a quilted warmer over the teapot – but something in the room had shifted as if we were in a painting and the artist had taken his brush to alter the canvas. We were all still there, filling our usual places in our usual spots, but the emotional threads that formed the background color had darkened imperceptibly. Just a shade, but we all felt it.

'Lord Byron told me that he has begun a new poem,' Shelley said, somewhat oblivious to the awkward pause in conversation.

'Indeed?' My interest kindled as I handed him a plate with thin slices of bread and butter.

'Not another one of those Turkish Tales – they are unworthy productions of his genius.' Mary passed on the refreshment since her appetite seemed to come and go during the day, but she poured herself a cup of tea. '*The Corsair* was written in less than a week – not the kind of work one expects from the author of *Childe Harold*—'

'It sold ten thousand copies in one day,' I protested, glaring at her. 'So it cannot be all bad.'

Mary shrugged. 'Sales are not always an indicator of quality. Why, look at the novels of Maria Edgeworth – such drivel.'

'Yet that "drivel" does pay one's rent,' Shelley added with a wry twist to his mouth. 'Sadly, I can only write what the Muse directs me to put to paper, but I certainly would not be averse to selling more than a handful of copies. Unless we use them to start fires, they provide little sustenance to our lives.'

'How true.' I sighed. We had barely enough money to pay for lodgings and food. I had almost depleted my small savings and Mary had none, so we depended on Shelley's incessant demands to his father for funds, and *he* was not happy with his only son's elopement. Not to mention, Sir Timothy had a reputation for being tight with the purse strings in general, though he had reluctantly agreed to a thousand pounds a year for us since William's birth.

'Perhaps I could do some copy work for an aristocrat with inclinations to write?' I proposed with a smile.

'Excellent idea. Did you have a particular lord in mind? Someone who might be working on a new poem?' He cast an ironic glance in my direction.

'Maybe.' What better way to make myself indispensable to him *and* provide a few pounds for us to survive in Geneva? It was not an expensive place to live, like London, so it would not take much for us to rent a cottage of our own.

'That is provided that Lord Byron decides to remain in the area for any length of time. His traveling companion, Doctor Polidori, told me they were making their way south to Italy – Venice, I think.' Shelley must have seen my crestfallen expression, and he added hastily, 'But I may have heard that incorrectly.'

'I couldn't blame him for not wanting to stay here with the

unrelenting gray skies and rain,' Mary commented, gazing out of the window. 'It feels like a shadowy blanket covers us at times. To think that horrible volcano is causing all of this – it is the stuff of nightmares.'

'But one wakes to a new dawn afterwards,' I chimed in, feeling certain that Byron meant to stay the summer in Geneva.

A shadow of doubt flitted across Mary's face and, for some reason, it irritated me.

Could she not be happy because I was happy?

'Maybe we can offer Lord Byron an incentive to stay.' Shelley held up his volume of Aeschylus. 'I had the sense that he is a man who likes a good literary debate – that could be quite stimulating and illuminating. I shall mark my favorite passages for our after-dinner discussion tonight and engage him with the beauties of our ancient Greek poet.'

I clapped my hands in gratitude.

And I could offer him other enticements.

Feeling quite light-hearted, I retreated to my room to dash off a letter to Byron. Hunting through the small desk for my quill and paper, I spied that the lid of my correspondence box stood ajar. I peeped inside, but the neat stack of letters seemed intact. Still, a thread of caution wafted through me – a hint of something being amiss.

Had someone been searching through my letters?

Two hours later, Byron sent his servant, Fletcher, with a message that he had secured a room on the lower floor of the hotel for supper – it had privacy and a view of the lake. I could barely contain my excitement, though it took some coaxing for Mary to abandon her forebodings about leaving William with a servant for the evening. Eventually, I found a local young woman of good reputation to stay with him, and Mary agreed.

Shelley decided to spend the afternoon reading poetry, so I proposed that Mary and I take William for a long walk through the winding streets of Geneva, just across the Pont du Mont Blanc – a bridge that connected our part of Geneva with the Old Town. After tea, we set out, ignoring the slight drizzle. It was a steep climb to the Place du Bourg-de-Four – the highest point in the city – while managing William's

baby carriage, but we wanted to see St Peter's Cathedral where
the Protestant reformer, John Calvin, preached in the sixteenth
century, or so Shelley told us. Standing in front of its neoclas-
sical facade, the rain had turned to a mild mist, and the breeze
coming in off the lake felt cool through my cotton dress. But
I did not care – the history and view of the lake were beyond
splendid.

'Are you not inspired by the beauty of this spot?' I murmured
as we scanned the cathedral's Doric columns and immense
wooden doors.

'More like awed . . . they say there is a chair inside where
Calvin reposed before he took the pulpit.'

'Not a seat that our dear Shelley would want to see,' I
teased.

She cast a droll look in my direction, but then a middle-aged
woman carrying a basket of ripe strawberries approached us with
a deep frown, and Mary's light mood instantly dissipated.

'I feel as if people are watching us now that Byron has
attached himself to our party,' she whispered, drawing back
from the old woman who hobbled past us, mumbling something
in French under her breath.

'He is quite famous, but we cannot let ourselves become too
agitated,' I urged, though I, too, had some misgivings, especially
after seeing my correspondence box disturbed last night. It had
never occurred to me that Byron's notoriety might have an effect
on our lives – might even cause a stranger to search through
our possessions for something connected to him.

'That is easier said than done, my dear Claire.' Mary leaned
down and tucked William's blanket tighter around his tiny
figure. 'We must not give rise to further gossip.'

Quickly, we made our way back to the Hotel d'Angleterre,
not speaking of the subject again, but the seeds of caution had
been planted. I kept my suspicions about my letters to myself.

By evening, we had regained some of our spirits as we sat
around a resplendent table (though Byron and Shelley
consumed little beyond vegetables and wine in Seltzer water)
in one of the hotel's private dining rooms; it contained a lofty
ceiling painted with picturesque scenes of sailing vessels skimming along the water on a sun-drenched day. One side of the

room was lined with windows from ceiling to floor that overlooked Lake Geneva, and in the twilight I noted that a heavy
fog obscured the mountains off to the east.

We all relaxed in the beauty of our surroundings and the
seclusion of our dining room in the cozy, flickering candlelight.

'Mary and I roamed through the old section of Geneva today
and saw the great cathedral – it was quite impressive,' I
informed the group in a light tone.

'Ah, yes. St Peter's Cathedral – the church of John Calvin.'
Byron made a sweeping motion with his hand, then turned to
Shelley. 'You may not be aware of this, but I was raised a
Calvinist in my early years in Scotland – a religion that promises
little hope or redemption in its gospel.'

'How unfortunate,' Shelley said.

Byron laughed. 'I think I earned the damnation that I was
predestined to enjoy.'

Polidori tipped his wine glass, causing a scarlet stain to
appear on the white linen tablecloth. Blood red.

'Clumsy boy,' Byron mocked as he refilled his physician's
glass.

'I enjoyed the outing, but we had the oddest feeling that
we were being watched,' Mary chimed in, a lovely vision in
the candlelight with her pale face and white silk dress.

Byron threw his table napkin over the stain. 'Your imagin-
ations may have been overstimulated, but I do not doubt the
occasional passer-by may cast a curious glance in your direction. They appear avidly interested in my movements – prying,
staring and gossiping. It never ceases – day and night. And
now that we are friends, you will be subject to the same treat-
ment. It can drive you mad – a subject fit only for a Roman
poet, eh, Shelley?'

'Most certainly not!' Shelley exclaimed. 'The Roman poets
cannot touch the transcendence of the Greeks – not on any
subject. They exalted freedom of thought and literature, which
set the world on its present course of constantly evolving
upwards toward an ever more ideal state—'

'My dear Shelley, you could not be more deluded.' Byron
fingered the stem of his crystal glass. 'The Greeks lived in a
fantasy world, believing that their little experiment in democracy

would change the world; it did not. By the time their city states fell and Rome became the dominant power in the world, our fate was set. Humanity will be engulfed time and time again with the endless cycle of tyranny, revolution, change – and tyranny once more. It was ever thus.'

Shelley shook his head in vigorous denial.

At least we had moved off the topic of being spied upon.

'I take it, then, my lord, that you are a cynic about human nature,' Mary added, placing her hands on the table and leaning forward. 'How do you explain the glorious French Revolution and the fall of aristocratic power? The common man never had such an opportunity to take his place at the table of abundance.'

'And what did he do with such opportunity?' Byron responded. 'Squander it away with the Terror – and eventually yet another tyranny with that power-mongering little Corsican, Napoleon, who picked up the crown of France with his sword and engulfed Europe in the worst war it has ever seen. No, I see nothing glorious in the Revolution when one tyrant was replaced by another . . .'

'Surely you see some redeeming quality in the French cause?' I posed.

'None whatsoever.' He took a deep swallow of the red wine – tossed it back without savoring. *A drink to forget.*

'Oh, come now, even you cannot discount the momentous event of destroying the French monarchy,' Shelley protested, his voice growing shrill with the passion of conviction. 'When Louis and Marie Antoinette died at the guillotine, the world held its breath and history was forever changed – for the good.' He pounded the table with his fist. 'I cannot believe otherwise.'

'Trust me, the aristocrats will be back,' Byron cut in with a voice that held a note of weariness. 'When that collective breath is finally and fully exhaled again now that Napoleon has been captured, those who did not die in the Terror will reclaim their birthright. Never underestimate the cunning of bluebloods; they find a way to survive like the cockroach lurking in the cellar, just waiting to reemerge.'

'You speak from such vast experience, my lord?' Polidori

shifted in his chair, nervously tapping his fingers on the table almost as if he wanted to provoke Byron. 'After all, you are a peer of the realm.'

'Indeed.' Byron rose to his feet and limped over to the immense windows, gazing out at the growing darkness. 'I have no illusions that I am not a part of the hypocrisy that I detest. I gave my speech to Parliament in support of the frame breakers – it made headlines but little difference in their lives. They will continue to experience privation and hardship and death – and no one will care. The privileged few will fight to maintain their ascendency.' He turned back to our little group with a twisted smile. 'But why should I, too, suffer? I experienced enough of genteel poverty when I was growing up in Edinburgh to know that I never want to live like that again. I intend to take up the good old virtue of avarice in my old age.'

'At not yet thirty?' I posed in disbelief.

'It's not actual years that age us; it's our actions, our lives . . . and lost loves.' He seated himself again, pouring another glass of wine. His features clouded with despair. 'If I had to calculate my age by that method, I would be over a hundred . . . I have made such an appalling mess of my life.'

Was he referring to the scandal of his divorce and the rumors of his illicit relationship with his half-sister, Augusta? I knew his marriage had been a sham; he told me as much when we met secretly in London. As for Augusta, I was never able to summon the courage to ask him because I feared the answer.

'I shall buy you a strongbox to hold your money, my lord, and a packet of hair dye, should you want to play the vain gentleman,' Shelley proposed with a smile. 'Or perhaps the real secret is to associate only with old men who keep tight purse strings – then you will always seem young and generous.'

Byron blinked, then began to chuckle deep in his chest. 'You mock me, sir, and I deserve it. What kind of host am I to depress my guests with such talk? This is an evening to celebrate the beginning of a friendship, not remember the end of a life that I can never have again. Such is the world.'

'And we must always believe that it will improve if we hold true to our ideals.' Shelley raised his wine glass. 'Shall we drink to life, love and beauty?'

We all raised our glasses in response, murmuring in agreement.

'And to new friends,' Byron added, glancing from person to person around the table, 'who brighten even the darkest hour.' I did the same, panning from Shelley's eager, open countenance, to Mary's hesitant expression, to Byron's flushed cheeks, ending with Polidori's fixation on . . . me. A twinge of fear passed through me at his constant monitoring. Why was he observing my every move?

Nervously, my eyes came back to Byron. Surely he would protect me. As if he had read my thoughts, his hand reached out under the table and found my knee, caressing my skin through the soft silk of my pink evening dress. My body melted inside, desire radiating through my veins. I'd missed the touch of his hands so dearly . . . and the passion-filled nights we had shared in England. My mad hope that he felt the same was turning to reality tonight. It was not just a passing fling but real, deep love.

I cast aside my suspicions about Polidori as fanciful imaginings.

We all clinked our glasses with a harmonious chime of crystal, and it felt like a beginning – a moment when the universe brought our little group together with the promise of a life-altering connection. It was as if a charmed circle had descended on us, sprinkling the magic of creative energy among us.

I believed that I would partake in the enchantment and take my place as an equal partner in the circle of friends, writing my way toward acceptance and maybe even fame.

And I hoped that Byron would be happy that I was expecting his child.

By the time we returned to our rooms, our feelings were soaring with the exhilaration of being in Byron's company. In spite of his occasional moodiness, his conversation had the effervescence of champagne: delicious and sparkling. We did an impromptu dance as I sang one of Shelley's favorite Irish songs, until he and Mary broke away to check on William. I sailed into my room as if on a cloud until I saw what lay on the floor. Then my breath caught in my throat at the sight.

My gold heart-shaped locket, supposedly given to my mother

by my unknown father, had been broken apart, the diamond chip missing and the pieces strewn about. Slowly, I bent down and scooped up the fragments, trying to piece them back together.

Did I have a thief – or an enemy?

Miss Eliza's Weekly Fashion and Gossip Pamphlet
May 30, 1816, Geneva

The Ladies' Page

Rumor has reached the ears of your editor, Miss Eliza, that the infamous poet, George Gordon, Lord Byron, has engaged a splendid house in Cologny – the Villa Diodati, which once housed the Puritan bard, John Milton. Oh, the irony!

I know all of you, my dear readers, are consumed by two burning questions: does Lord Byron intend to linger on the shores of Lake Geneva, and does he intend to reside at the villa alone?

If you recall, ladies, Lord Byron has recently separated from his wife, Miss Annabella Milbank, and departed from England under a cloud of scandal (which I cannot print here, of course). Perhaps he intends to partake of our lovely Genevan society for the entire summer? If so, you can be certain that I will find a way to meet him and delve into his future plans.

One last juicy tidbit: Lord Byron has been seen in the company of Percy Bysshe Shelley, the son of Sussex land-owner, Sir Timothy Shelley . . . and two as yet unnamed women (shocking!). Is it possible that there is love in the air – or debauchery?

Ladies, take your spyglasses and fix them on the Villa Diodati.

THREE

Florence, Italy, 1873

I could scarcely breathe as I came back to the present in Florence.

Glancing down at my wrinkled hands, though, was a potent reminder of the intervening years.

Remembering that first night when we were all together in Geneva during the summer of 1816 stirred up deeper, more disturbed memories than I had allowed myself to recall for many, many years. In spite of the excitement of our first meeting on the lake and the intimate connections that immediately sprang up as we bonded over politics and poetry, there were shadows around us right from the beginning.

The incessant storms, the ailing health of little William who was destined to die so young . . . and Polidori – always lurking in the background like a dark cloud.

I had also forgotten about my correspondence box and broken locket, because nothing had ever been tampered with again. None of my letters actually turned out to be missing, and I had the locket fixed, as well as the tiny diamond replaced, without mentioning either incident to anyone. I did not think anyone would believe me since I was known for my high spirits.

Later on that summer, other events occurred that made these early ones pale in comparison.

But I was not ready to resurrect those memories yet . . .

Glancing down at the note that had been folded under my teacup, I read once more: *Your daughter lives.*

Was it possible someone in that group had deceived me all along? Stolen from me? Maybe even worked against me after I had given birth to Byron's daughter, Allegra?

The walls of my bedroom seemed to close in and, all at once, the silence felt oppressive, as if the past had reached forward and seized my chest, squeezing the air from my lungs. I sat back against the pillows and took in several deep breaths, calming myself.

Perhaps the note was someone's idea of a jest. A sick, twisted one, certainly, but a joke nonetheless. My family and close friends all knew that even though I had received a death certificate from the nuns at the convent, I had never actually seen Allegra's body. Yet, surely, the nuns would not have lied. Now that I had converted to Catholicism and conversed with holy sisters in Florence, I knew the power of what it meant when a woman dedicated her life to the service of God.

Besides, even if there had been a sliver of doubt about Allegra's fate, why contact me now? Who would want to stir up these feelings in a woman of my age? Even more disturbing, did the note have something to do with Mr Rossetti's appearance? It hardly seemed a coincidence.

Thoughts racing, I eased myself into a sitting position to massage my ankle as I tried to gather my scattered thoughts into the deductive processes that Shelley had taught me from his favorite philosopher, Aristotle.

Fact: my illegitimate daughter, Allegra, had been born during the autumn of 1816; her father was Lord Byron and he had taken over her upbringing since he could provide for her financially when I could not (well . . . a *little* emotion had crept in).

Fact: our small, tight circle in Geneva knew about Allegra; Shelley had even helped to negotiate my agreement with Byron concerning my daughter's future.

Fact: Byron, Shelley, Mary, Polidori and I were the main players in that summer of literary (and passionate) pursuits.

Fact: Allegra had died in the Convent at Bagnacavallo on April 2, 1822 – at the age of five years and three months. She was buried in an unmarked grave outside Harrow Church near Byron's ancestral home in England – sadly, the churchwardens would permit no memorial tablet to Byron's illegitimate child inside the church (or so I was told).

Tears welled up in my eyes – reason and logic be damned. The thought of my little child lying in her cold grave could still cause a grief so deep and profound that it felt as if I were falling from a mountaintop into an emotional abyss that had no bottom.

I gave myself a mental shake, pulling myself back into reality, if not sanity.

Someone wanted me to believe that Allegra was still alive, and I had to find out who was responsible for sending me that note – and why it appeared the day Mr Rossetti came to call to tell me that I had become a footnote in history and he wanted to remedy that injustice. By purchasing my letters.

Perplexing.

A tiny voice then whispered inside of me: *Perhaps Allegra is alive.*

Before I could stop myself, hope sprang up, unbidden as the flowering of a rose in spring.

I did not know how it could be possible, but I knew I had to find out once and for all – perhaps even atone for having handed her over to her father in her youth and allowing him to install her in a convent school when she was but five years old.

Redemption.

In my mind's eye, I could see Allegra as a child of two years when I first took her sea-bathing in Dover on an unseasonably warm day with Shelley and Mary, who had William with them. I heard my daughter's laughter ring out, just at the moment that a seabird dipped low and seized a fish in its beak. Clapping her hands, she tottered toward the surf, and I caught her up in my arms to keep her safe from the swiftly moving tide. Allegra's dazzling blue eyes and soft curls shone on the sun-drenched beach, and I was lost in the most complete and utter love for my child, even as I traveled to Italy to surrender her to her father.

Oh, my dear, sweet Allegra. I miss you even now . . .

'Aunt Claire, do you want to have tea now?'

I spied Paula in the doorway, arms folded, with a frown of concern on her face. 'Mr Rossetti left thirty minutes ago because he thought you were too weak to continue your conversation. Apparently, he also had to meet someone at Santa Croce to discuss selling a painting. I looked in a few minutes ago, and I thought you had fallen asleep.'

'No, I was just resting.' Summoning a smile of reassurance, I continued, 'Did anyone else enter my bedroom today, aside from Raphael?' I asked.

'Not that I know.' Her eyes widened in caution. 'Why do you ask? Is something missing? If so, I will immediately ask him to question the cook. She came to us with good references from the landlord, but we really do not know her—'

'Nothing is missing,' I cut into this train of thought swiftly and firmly. 'I was just curious because my . . . my stack of books seemed to be out of order earlier. I always place Byron's poems on top, but then again I may have removed the volume myself after we looked at it the other day and later reinserted it in the middle of the pile . . .' Babbling away, I swung my feet to the floor and stood up slowly, testing out my weight on the sore ankle. It held. 'I will have tea in the sitting room after all; my ankle seems much better after resting today, though my memory seems to have taken a turn for the worse.' *To say the least.* It was time to take charge of this situation – even at my advanced age, I was not done yet. And I could not share any of my suspicions with Paula yet, for her sake.

'The blue-flowered china teapot?' she queried.

'Yes, my dear.' It was the one that we had used daily in Geneva; I could not part with it – ever. 'And please do not concern yourself with my silly query about books in my bedroom. I must be going dotty to have thought someone entered our rooms without our knowledge. Imagine that?' I gave a light flip of my hand.

'Hardly.' Paula dropped a light kiss on my head, and I patted her hand with a twinge of guilt at my dissembling act.

I would find the truth – no matter what.

After an early dinner of pasta *fagioli* soup – and small talk about Mr Rossetti's good manners and kind attitude – I feigned a sudden bout of weariness and retreated to my room. Paula settled me on my chaise longue, my ankle again cushioned on a pillow, and I waved her off with a grateful smile.

After she exited and closed the door, I immediately rose and hobbled over to my empire mahogany writing desk. It was positioned near the large window that faced the Boboli

Gardens and held my treasures: a few pieces of jewelry (including the repaired locket), a small sketch of Allegra, and my precious letters from the summer of 1816 – and the later years in Italy.

Perhaps I would find something in the latter that I had overlooked all of these years. A clue. A reference. Anything that might point to Allegra being alive.

I unlocked the top drawer and gently slid out several stacks of correspondence.

Slipping on a pair of spectacles, I unfolded each yellowed letter and scanned the contents slowly, carefully. The words brought back my daily activities of that time, some of which were exciting, such as sailing to different spots around Lake Geneva to see medieval towns and explore crumbling castles. But much of my correspondence centered on the mundane: copy work that I did for Byron, readings that I completed under Shelley's tutelage and strolls that I took through the open markets to find the cheapest food. Living for love and poetry still required money – even residing in our tiny cottage near the lake. Of course, when we dined at the Villa Diodati with Byron – which we did often – it was a completely different situation: we had access to every dish we could ask for, as well as copious amounts of wine, though Shelley rarely partook of rich food.

Byron could be petty, harsh even, but he was always generous to friends.

Speak of the devil . . . I pulled out a thin stack of correspondence, folded neatly and tied with a red ribbon. My letters from Byron. My letters *to* Byron – most of which had been returned to me, unopened. I didn't need to look at the second group; I knew those appeals by heart since I had rewritten them in my head many, many times, wondering if there was something I could have said or done to keep our love intact. Later, all I wanted was Allegra, and that did not happen, either.

Toying with the ribbon for a few moments, I finally untied the knot with a trembling hand. Sorting through my returned communiques – one by one – I checked the dates. After I had returned to England in the autumn of 1816 to give birth to our child, I had written to Byron repeatedly, but to no avail.

Shelley had become our intermediary by that time, and he had handled most of the arrangements about our daughter's future.

I sighed.

Scant communication with Byron had left me anxious and bitter, and my tone grew increasingly demanding in the years after Allegra's birth. I winced at the raw emotion in sentence after sentence, which did nothing but push Byron further away. How foolish of me, but I was young and angry.

Then, in midsummer 1821, Byron finally responded to my appeals to see Allegra after he had placed her in school at the Capuchin Convent of Bagnacavallo.

My heartbeat quickened slightly as I unfolded the letter and spied the bold handwriting scrawled across the page.

> Ravenna, 1821
> Dear Claire,
>
> I am glad you are well and residing with the Shelleys at Leghorn, enjoying the beauties of the Adriatic. I was even more delighted to learn that you are taking swimming lessons – it is certainly one of my greatest pleasures.
>
> On a more disagreeable note, I cannot honor your request to visit Allegra or have her brought to my residence here in Ravenna. Shelley can attest that my situation is not conducive to [blackened words] a young child. Unfortunately, we live in a world where the most innocent can be prey to serpents in the garden . . .
>
> *A presto,*
> B.

Slowly, I lowered the letter to my lap and glanced out of the window, mulling over each and every word. Shelley had visited Byron in Ravenna and taken my letter with him, requesting that Allegra be removed from the convent. I did not believe she was happy there and proposed that Allegra live with him again – as he had promised before she was born. More than anything, I wanted to see her, hold her in my arms and stroke her soft curls. Just once. If only once.

Was that too much for a mother to ask?

But I had received only this short note in response. No other letters passed between us until after Allegra's death.

Adjusting my spectacles, I scanned the missive again, pausing this time over the blackened words. I had always assumed that section was a simple mistake that he had crossed out, but now I found myself fixating on the missing words. What if he had deliberately deleted words because he didn't want to arouse my alarm about Allegra's situation?

I held the parchment sheet up to the window, trying to make out what was under the blackened section. Squinting in the quickly fading sunlight, I still could not see anything beyond black ink strikeout. Then I picked up a small letter opener and scratched at the darkened spot. Two tiny flakes dropped off, and a jolt of excitement rose up inside me. It might work. I kept rubbing at the ink with a light, feathery motion and, gradually, the ink chipped away to reveal the words underneath: my situation is not conducive to *the safety of* a young child.

Sitting back, I blinked. Why had he struck through the words? And why would Allegra not have been *safe* with him?

Granted, Byron had been living in Ravenna at the time with his Italian mistress and her hothead brother, known for his revolutionary beliefs. But Byron was an English lord and, as such, untouchable in Italy no matter what the opinions of his inamorata's brother. Allegra would have always been safe with him. Was he simply being overly cautious because Italy was then a divided country caught in a post-Napoleonic power struggle? I vaguely recollected that a battle had occurred near Naples that spring . . . and the Neapolitans had been defeated, but the military rout was far south and had little impact on the northern regions.

Our lives had continued, untouched by Italian politics.

Or at least as far as I remembered. Sadly, I was young and preoccupied with my own life, and paid little attention to the events swirling around our little expatriate group. Byron had obviously felt the convent in Bagnacavallo was preferable to Ravenna, though it was scarcely eleven kilometers to the west. I assumed at the time that he did not want to be bothered with the care of a young child, but maybe other forces had been at work behind his decision.

Slipping off my spectacles, I rubbed my eyes. Did any of this really matter? Or connect to the note that I found today? It was so long ago, and since I was one of the few members of our circle who was still alive, I had no one else to ask – except Trelawny. I vowed to write to him before the week was out to see if he recalled anything unusual about Allegra's . . . demise.

I stared down at Byron's letter again, the writing now blurry to my old eyes, but the words kept echoing through my mind. *Her safety.* Allegra's safety. We had all failed to keep her safe in one way or another.

Shuffling through the rest of my letters, I double-checked to see if I had any further communications from Byron during the last half of 1821. I did not. Nor did I possess a single letter from the Mother Superior at the convent. Just a huge, empty silence in terms of my daughter's welfare before her death.

A quiet knock at the door interrupted my search, and I ceased all activity.

'Aunt Claire?' Paula prompted, without opening the door. 'Are you awake?'

I didn't respond.

She called out my name again and, after a few moments, I heard her heels moving off on the hard stone floor.

Still not ready to share with her my suspicions about Mr Rossetti or the note about Allegra, I knew I had to find more concrete information before I brought my niece into any of the developments today – too much was at stake.

Yet, as vague and disturbing as the last two days had been, they had also ignited something in my life that had been missing for years: a flicker of optimism about the future. It might not be burning brightly yet, but the embers had been stirred.

I arranged the Byron letters into a little pile, retied them with the ribbon and then placed them with the rest of my cherished correspondence inside the desk drawer and locked it again, leaving out the note from Ravenna. It was time to plan my next move before I saw Mr Rossetti once more. But I needed time to rest and think.

Returning to my bed, I rang a little silver bell and Paula immediately thrust open the door, Georgiana at her side. 'Are you feeling better?' Her daughter started to dash in my direction, but Paula held her back.

'Somewhat, my dear, but I may turn in early – it has been quite an eventful day.' I smiled at both of them.

'Did Mr Rossetti upset you?' Paula queried, looking down briefly. 'Because if the thought of selling some of your letters is a prospect that causes you too much distress, I think we should reconsider the entire thing. And do not worry – we will find another way to bring in more funds. While you were resting, I spoke with Raphael, and he suggested that I might take in sewing for some of the local Florentine ladies—'

'We are not that desperate yet,' I interrupted with a firm tone. 'In truth, while it was somewhat . . . unsettling to revisit the past, I am resolved that it may hold the key to our future well-being.' I did not lie – exactly.

Paula frowned. 'It is *your* decision, Aunt.'

'I know.' Extending my hand to sweet Georgiana, she pulled at her mother's retraining grasp in my direction. 'Please leave her with me for a little while. I need to hear her laughter and bask in her love.'

Releasing her daughter, who bounded towards me, Paula turned away, then she looked back in my direction. 'I cannot tell you how much you mean to us.'

'Nor I you.'

Paula gave a quick nod and disappeared as Georgiana happily settled on to the bed next to me. Holding out her book, she asked, 'Would you read to me, Auntie? I cannot make out some of the words.'

'Of course I will, my dear.' Opening the book, I glanced down at her cornflower-blue eyes – so sweet and trusting – and my arm tightened protectively around her tiny shoulders. 'Sometimes stories can be confusing if we do not know the right questions – or right person – to ask.'

She sighed in contentment as I started reciting the children's book aloud.

I knew where *I* would begin to find some answers tomorrow. The note had stirred up doubts about Allegra's fate, and I needed to put them to rest before I could sell Mr Rossetti my letters and let the past go.

I needed to see Father Gianni.

After a good night's rest, I awakened the next morning with a renewed sense of purpose. I tested out my ankle upon rising and found it surprisingly stable – certainly strong enough to do what I had in mind. Throwing open my shutters to a sunny Florentine summer day, I managed to complete my toilette unassisted. And by mid-morning I was enjoying a light break-fast of butter-flavored porridge in the kitchen with Paula as I declared my intention to go to the Basilica di San Lorenzo to see Father Gianni, my priest.

Paula cast a startled glance in my direction. 'Are you certain that you want to exert yourself like that? Is your ankle strong enough?'

'It is much better today – as you can see.' I rose to my feet and circled around the small oak table with slow, careful steps. 'Indeed, I think the fresh air will be most beneficial for my physical recovery, but I also feel the need for spiritual guid-ance right now. Mr Rossetti's visit has shaken me a bit, and I could use Father Gianni's wisdom at this time.' Seating myself again, I continued, 'Raphael will hire a carriage to take me there, and I promise to walk only as far as the Old Chapel in the basilica—'

Uncertainty shadowed her features, and I leaned over to place my hand on hers in reassurance. 'I promise not to over-exert myself.'

'I suppose if the driver waits for you, it will be all right,' she finally said. 'But you must return before the heat becomes too intense. It is going to be quite warm today.'

Squeezing her fingers in agreement, I fastened my glance on hers. 'Once I have a chance to sort through matters with Father Gianni, I will send a note to Mr Rossetti about a second meeting, but only after you and I discuss the next move . . .'

She laughed. 'You make it sound like a chess game, Aunt.'

'Is not everything in life?'

'Perhaps.'

Her puzzlement caused me to add hastily, 'We must make

sure that we receive proper payment for my letters.' Well . . . it was partially true.

Just then, Raphael strolled into the kitchen with a basket that contained two loaves of fresh-baked bread from the market, filling the kitchen with the delightful smell of rosemary and garlic. As he set the basket on a nearby counter, Paula's glance moved in his direction with a softening of her eyes that spoke of a deeper affection than I had previously seen. Or perhaps I had not really noted it until I began thinking about my youthful romance yesterday. *She loves him.* Then he turned and smiled, his expression mirroring hers, his dark eyes filled with a depth of feeling that seemed to rival my niece's emotions.

Ah, the sweetness of two souls finding themselves in the world. Could anything be more beautiful?

Yet his young face held a sadness that beclouded his love. Or did it hint at something else?

Then I glanced at Raphael's slim physique in his rough black breeches and plain white cotton shirt. Poverty held him in sway, as well. In fact, his financial straits were even more desperate than ours – he worked for our landlord and picked up odd jobs throughout the city. But it was not enough if he chose eventually . . . to marry.

I had not seen it before but, in that instant, I realized that Paula and Raphael would never have a future together unless something changed in our fortunes – and soon. The last thing I wanted to do was place obstacles in the way of young lovers. I knew the deep despair of not being able to share my life with the man who was my heart's most cherished desire – a loss that followed me through the rest of my days. Perhaps I had been too young, too impulsive when I fell madly in love, but I never regretted pursuing passion over reason.

Paula *must* have a chance for that kind of life with Raphael – no matter if it lasted only a short time. She and Raphael, along with dear Georgiana. They would be a family and live the life that I had always wanted.

Clearing my throat deliberately, I stood once more. 'Raphael, would you please hire a carriage for me? I need to see Father Gianni this morning.'

'*Che cosa?*' He shot a quick look at Paula, who gave a brief nod of assent. Then he shrugged and strode off, murmuring something in Italian under his breath that I did not catch – probably a reference to the eccentricities of old age – but he complied nonetheless.

'At least let me accompany you, Aunt Claire,' my niece posed. 'I would feel better if I were with you—'

'No need, my dear. If I tire, I shall simply have the driver bring me home.' I gave her a quick pat and headed toward my room before she could fashion yet another protest. She would not deter me from my mission.

An hour later, my open carriage was making its way through the narrow, crooked streets of Florence, its wooden wheels thumping over the old, uneven cobblestones. Angling my parasol to shield my face from the sun, I nodded at one or two female acquaintances standing near the Uffizi Gallery as we passed by its stately pillars. They smiled and I did the same, but the exchange had no warmth of friendship – only polite civility, knowing they probably gossiped afterwards about my outdated striped calico gown and matching bonnet.

I did not particularly care, especially this morning. I was on a quest. As we drove toward the Duomo, the streets were semi-deserted, with only morning delivery carts unpacking foods and sundries in front of various small shops.

Florentine mornings possessed a lovely charm: the quiet business of a city preparing for the heat and crowds of midday. I enjoyed watching the craftsmen setting out gold filigree jewelry on the Ponte Vecchio and farmers stacking ripe vegetables in the open markets – row upon row of large crates. The whole tableau of vivid colors and aromatic smells extended across the web-like network of main streets and, beyond them, the alleyways held whispers and echoes of past famous and powerful residents' hidden secrets. I embraced it all as part of the city of dreams.

The carriage slowed down as we circled around the Piazza del Duomo with its massive cathedral rising up in the center in all its medieval splendor – a green, white and pink marble facade adorned by stained-glass windows. The essence of art and religion – everything that Florence stood for and I believed in when I made this city my last residence and Catholicism my faith. *Beauty is truth, truth beauty.* And ever was it so.

All of a sudden, the carriage halted and I realized that we had reached the Basilica di San Lorenzo – the Medicis' church. More modest than the magnificent Duomo on the outside, the church's facade had never actually been finished; it had a rough-hewn appearance, but it also housed a magnificent interior. The main draw for me, though, was my parish priest, Father Gianni – my dearest friend.

The driver helped me out of the carriage, and I asked him to wait. Then I entered the massive front door and immediately felt the cool serenity of the basilica with its thick walls and slate-colored columned arcades. As I made my way past the benches toward the high altar, I spied Father Gianni standing near the bronze pulpit. At my approach, he broke into a warm smile and extended his hands to cover mine.

'Signora Clairmont, I am delighted that you are up and about again. *Bene. Molto bene.*' Almost my age, Father Gianni had a shock of gray hair, thick brows and the benign expression of a man who extended kindness to all. He was the one person whom I trusted in the world – and I knew he would help me.

'May I talk with you for a few minutes – not as my confessor, but as my friend?' I placed my hand on his arm. 'It's urgent.'

'By all means.' His features knit in puzzlement as he gestured toward one of the benches. We sat down, both facing forward. 'What brings you here today?'

I stared at the marble crucifix positioned above the altar and folded my hands in my lap. Then I began to speak, and I poured out the whole story of my lost daughter, including my illicit love affair with Byron, my break with Mary and my later life drifting around Europe as a governess. I ended with Rossetti's visit and the mysterious note about Allegra being alive. Even as I related the events, I feared seeing disapproval creep into his face since I had never summoned the courage before to tell him about my early life.

But Father Gianni simply listened. Occasionally, he prompted me with a question or two, then fell silent when I finished.

'Do you believe this man Rossetti might know about your daughter's fate?' he finally asked.

'Possibly. I know nothing about him. An old friend, Edward Trelawny, wrote to me a few days ago, saying that Mr Rossetti was interested in purchasing my letters.'

He rubbed his chin meditatively. 'It would be quite a coincidence that the note appeared on the very day he called, though he said nothing to you about it?'

'No.'

'I will make inquiries about him,' he said in a firm voice. 'We need to know first if he is an honest man—'

'But what about my daughter? Do you think it possible that she did not die in the convent at Bagnacavallo? I saw the death certificate a few weeks after her death, but it was lost during the years of my travels.' My voice rose in an excited pitch. 'Could it have been . . . forged?'

A window rattled, and I jumped.

'It was just the wind – nothing more,' he reassured me in a low voice. 'The year she died was a chaotic time for *Italia*, especially in Ravenna with rumors about the Carbonari revolutionaries plotting an uprising, but I might be able to locate some old records that the church preserved.' He motioned his head in the direction of the Laurentian Library, adjacent to the basilica. It was the great *biblioteca* of Florence that housed documents from all of Italy. 'If any information exists about the convent and your daughter's fate, I will find it. Trust me.'

'*Grazie*, Father.' I exhaled in relief as I handed him Byron's letter from Ravenna.

'Let us pray together that God in His mercy will guide us in our search for the truth.' He bowed his head and murmured, 'But say nothing until I meet you here tomorrow at ten o'clock.'

I would be as silent as the grave.

After I took leave of Father Gianni, I had the driver take me home and I hobbled up the stairs to my apartment, feeling a wave of intense fatigue. When I reached the second floor where our rented rooms were located, I stood there for a few moments to catch my breath; it was early afternoon and growing warmer by the hour. Letting myself in, I called out for Paula but heard no response. Then I spied the note propped up on the fireplace mantle: *Went to the market with Georgiana – will return shortly.* I sighed with relief.

Her absence would give me time to rest and come up with a story that would explain the length of my visit with Father Gianni.

Easing myself into one of the aging throne-style chairs near the marble fireplace, I leaned back and closed my eyes. Certainly, I had always loved an adventure and it looked as if I might have one last exploit, but could I summon the energy to live it to the fullest?

Forse – perhaps.

At least Father Gianni believed in me. And, even more importantly, he believed that the note questioning Allegra's death had a sinister element about it – at best, an unsettling motivation.

Just then, I felt a hand touch my shoulder and I gasped. My eyelids fluttered open to the sight of Raphael with a glass of water in hand.

'Signora Claire – for you.' He held out a piece of crystal that was filled to the brim with clear, sparkling liquid.

'*Grazie mille.*' Taking the glass from him, I quickly swallowed most of its contents. 'I did not realize how thirsty I was.'

'You were gone a long time at confession,' he responded, looking down at me with a shuttered expression. Was he suspicious about my conversation with Father Gianni?

'Was I? At my age, one has many behaviors for which to atone.' Keeping my tone artless, I gestured toward the matching wingback across from me. 'Please, join me.'

He hesitated, then shrugged and sat down on the edge of the chair.

I sipped my water and watched him with a surreptitious glance. What did I really know about Raphael beyond the fact that he appeared to care deeply for Paula? Our landlord had recommended him to us a little over six months ago, and while he performed light tasks around the apartment, he spoke very little and revealed almost nothing of a personal nature.

Almost without volition, mistrust spread into the very air around me.

He was pleasing to the eye, for certain, in that Italian way that managed to look effortlessly masculine; his features could have been etched from one of the Roman statues that ringed the amphitheater in the gardens. *Un bel viso.* A handsome face, framed with dark, curly hair.

He turned his head, catching me in the act of studying him, and I blinked rapidly as a sudden flash of memory brought back the face of another man – the one who had captured my heart so long ago. Byron's face rose up in my mind – so sad and unhappy in the late-evening firelight in Geneva – as he recited lines from his latest poem. His voice deep and melodic. For just a moment, it felt as if a fissure of time had split open and Byron's features glossed over Raphael's – from a time when I was young, as well, still believing in the possibilities of life as I pursued an elusive dream of happiness . . .

But it never happened.

Byron's image instantly dissolved and I saw Raphael's face again – and only his.

'Signora?' He reached out and caught the glass as it started to slip out of my hand, causing a few drops of water to splash on the hard, unforgiving stone floor. 'Is your ankle causing you pain?'

'Just a bit.' I managed a small, tight smile as I took the glass from him and drained the rest of the cool liquid. 'I never asked about your family . . . Do they live in Florence?'

Raphael looked away for a few moments. 'No, my parents died in a carriage accident when I was a *bambino*. I never knew them – not even what they looked like. Because I was so young when I lost them, I did not mourn the loss of something that I never really possessed.' His voice was matter-of-fact as he related his story. 'My *nonna* raised me, but now she, too, is gone.'

'So you are all alone?'

'*Si.*'

'I suppose we have that in common, though my own mother disowned me and I never knew my father's identity. You and I have learned to rely on our own wits and the kindness of others.' I toyed with my crucifix pendant. 'Our landlord, Signor Ricci, thinks highly of you as he was the one who recommended your services to us—'

'He knew my *nonna*, but I had not seen him in several years since she died.' Raphael shifted in the chair, curling his fingers around the armrests. 'Signor Ricci sent word through a friend that you and your niece were seeking a local man to help out with your daily tasks. I needed the work. A man without a family in Italy has few options to make his way in the world.'

My suspicions about him abated somewhat. Perhaps that explained the sad tinge that I had noted on his face.

Raphael leaned forward, his elbows on his thighs and earnestness in his voice. 'I may have no family and no money, but I am loyal to you and Paula – to the end. I would do anything for her.'

'So you love my niece?' I raised my brows in inquiry.

'With all my heart,' he replied without hesitation.

'Truly? Would you sacrifice everything for her, no matter what?'

'Gladly.'

Raphael sat back and our conversation trailed off into silence.

Scarcely minutes later, Paula entered the apartment with Georgiana at her heels. When the little girl spied me, she darted in my direction. Raphael immediately rose to his feet as I folded my great-niece in my embrace.

'Auntie, look what Mama bought me.' Georgiana produced a tiny charm in the shape of a flower. 'Is it not pretty?'

'Indeed, my dear.'

Raphael took the shopping basket from Paula, their hands brushing. It was a brief touch, but I saw it and registered the flush of emotion on my niece's face – a delicate pink color that stained her cheeks.

'May I see it, *piccola*?'

Shyly, Georgiana held it up.

'Ah, it is the Florentine iris, the white flower of the city that grows wild in the hills above the river. Some say it symbolizes the goddess Iride; some say it represents the Virgin Mary – but who knows?' He rubbed her soft curls affectionately. 'It is enough simply to behold its beauty.' Raphael's glance transferred to Paula.

A touch of wonder came over Georgiana as she looked at the charm again, then she held it tightly to her chest.

'How was your time with Father Gianni?' Paula asked as she removed the wide-brimmed straw hat that she always wore during summer strolls to the open-air market. The Italian sun, though warm and inviting, was not kind to pale English skin. 'Did he help you to find the wisdom that you need?'

'Indeed, yes. Confession is good for the soul, as they say. He helped me to understand that the present is always tied to the past, and letting go of my mementos might be the best way to make peace—'

'With what?' Paula's brows knit in puzzlement.

'Illusions, fantasies – the things we cling to as we get older.' I tiptoed over my words as if I were making my way across a field of sharp, pointed rocks. 'There is no point in chasing rainbows . . . especially if I intend to sell my letters.' *Once I knew for certain about Allegra.*

'But that is what the iris means,' Raphael cut in excitedly. 'The goddess Iride was a messenger to the gods and brought them the rainbow – hope. *Speranza.*'

Paula laughed and shook her head. 'I have no idea what you both are talking about – let us have tea and stop all of this talk about goddesses and rainbows. Mr Rossetti will be expecting an answer from us soon, and you need to rest, Aunt Claire.' She ushered Raphael out of the room and Georgiana followed in their wake.

Mr Rossetti would have his answer – after I spoke with Father Gianni the following morning.

The next day, it had turned cloudy – a leaden sky with no hint of sun. But my ankle was getting stronger. I quickly donned my second-best green calico dress and enjoyed breakfast in my room, trying to avoid any unnecessary questioning from Paula. I was not sure how long I could keep hiding my true purpose for seeing Father Gianni, but once I had something concrete from him, I would no longer lie and dissemble to my own family.

Raphael had the same driver waiting outside our rooms, and I made my way out before my niece could query me.

Once I settled into the carriage, the driver turned to me, '*Signora, un carro ha bloccato il ponte.*' A wagon blocked the Ponte Vecchio.

I suggested the bridge further south, and he nodded. As we slowly moved forward, I looked up and saw Paula's surprised face in the window. She was mouthing words that I could not hear, but I pretended that she was wishing me a happy outing. I waved and smiled as I murmured 'Andiamo!' to the driver.

He tapped the horse lightly with his whip, and the carriage lurched forward with more speed. I tightened the strings of my bonnet as I focused on the road ahead, even when a gentle misting rain began. It didn't matter if it stained my green cotton dress or drenched my one good pair of shoes. Nothing mattered except what Father Gianni had to tell me.

We arrived at the Basilica di San Lorenzo right at the point the drizzle turned into a heavy downpour, and I hurried into the church, shaking off the raindrops as I removed my hat. The cool dampness of the ancient building was offset by a sweet scent of incense and the odor of warm wax from the altar candles. Inhaling deeply to draw in the comforting smells, I noted a few worshippers seated on the wooden benches, praying with their heads bowed as they held their rosary beads. Scanning the length of the room, I did not see Father Gianni anywhere near the high altar.

Nevertheless, I moved in that direction, registering the lyrical strains of a choir drifting from deep within the basilica. And the bells in the distance. Always the Florentine bells. I counted as they rang out across the Old City ten times – the appointed hour for Father Gianni to meet me, but he was nowhere to be seen.

Biting my lower lip nervously, I halted in front of the altar. Where was he? Had he forgotten his promise?

Or even worse: had something happened to him?

Feelings of alarm grew inside me as the minutes ticked by. *Let him come soon.* My ankle began to ache from the dank coolness rising up from the stone floor, but I dared not leave the spot. I could not and would not depart until I saw him. Reaching for the altar rail, I shifted my weight to the hard, solid piece of wood, clutching it with both hands to remain upright.

'Signora Clairmont?' Father Gianni appeared in the doorway to the left side of the high altar.

I exhaled in profound relief as I stretched my hands out to him. 'I am so happy to see you, Father.'

He clasped my fingers and gave me a wide smile. 'Did you think I had forgotten?'

'N–no, but I . . . I feared perhaps you had reconsidered or had become ill.' Even as I said the words, I shook off my fanciful imaginings.

'Come, let us sit down, and I will tell you what I found.' We strolled over to the front pew and sat down, side by side.

Once seated, I turned to him. 'I must know if Allegra survived.'

He paused. 'Let me tell you first what I *do* know: Mr Rossetti is an English tourist and quite respectable from what my sources could tell me. It is apparently true that he traveled here to meet you and purchase your letters.'

'And Allegra?'

'I found records in the *biblioteca* that Allegra Byron was placed in the Convent of Bagnacavallo in the spring of 1821, as you told me. Her name appears in the roll, along with about twelve other young girls who were the same age. Some of them were British and some were Italian. Nothing else was recorded in the provincial records except . . .' His voice trailed off.

'What?' My voice held a note of urgency.

'During April of 1822, typhus swept through the convent, and many children died—'

'Was Allegra one of them?' Deep sadness began to well up around my heart like a poisoned fountain, drowning all light and hope in bleakness. I had been a fool to even dare believe that my daughter had survived.

'It is likely she . . . succumbed to the disease,' he said, touching my arm. 'Very few children survived it in the convent.'

'But do you have proof?'

'Not exactly—'

'So then it *is* possible that she lived?'

Glancing down for a few moments, he patted my hand. 'If

she had survived the typhus, surely she would have been returned to her father. Did he not say at the time that she had died?'

'Not himself. I heard about her death from Shelley and Mary, though they hid it from me for five days after Byron sent word to them. They said they were waiting for the right time to give me the details, for my sake, but I never quite believed that. Then the death certificate came, but it was much later.' I remembered how Shelley had entered the room where I had been reading, his steps tentative and his face drawn tight with sadness. I knew bad news was coming, but I had never dreamed it would be the type that caused my world to stop.

'Why would you not believe them?'

'Just a feeling . . . I always thought that Byron asked them to wait, but I never could work out why. Now I have a reason to question his behavior. Perhaps she did not really die?' I ended on a question, but Father Gianni shook his head imperceptibly.

'Be careful not to give in to false hope,' he urged with gentle kindness. 'I have written to the Mother Superior at the convent to verify Allegra's death certificate and then, when I receive her response, I will send it to you as final proof of what happened to your daughter.' He paused. 'After that, there will be no question, but prepare yourself because I have no reason to believe that her fate was any different from what you have believed all of these years.'

I sat back, taking in his wise words. Of course, Father Gianni was right. I had let my emotions take me into a place of unfounded fantasies. Silly. Desperate. Foolish. 'I understand, Father, and thank you.' I began to rise, but he signaled for me to wait with a quick flick of his hand and I slid back down.

'One more thing . . . When I looked at the letter that Byron wrote from Ravenna, it had a faint image at the top. Had you noticed?'

'No.' My brows knit in puzzlement.

He retrieved the letter from his robe pocket, unfolded it and pointed at a small ink-drawn image of a bowl with a star etched on the front. 'See, right here?'

Squinting without my spectacles, I noted the drawing. 'I never really noticed it – just assumed it was an absent-minded mark he had drawn.'

'Perhaps it seemed that way to you, but Italians would immediately recognize it as a charcoal burner.'

I shrugged in helpless confusion.

'Let me explain it to you with something that I left on my desk.' He rose to his feet, still clutching the letter. 'Wait here and I will be back – *un momento.*'

'But . . .'

Ignoring my protestations, he quickly disappeared through the altar's side door.

Was Father Gianni showing the signs of his age? A silly drawing of a charcoal burner hardly seemed significant. All I wanted to know was whether Allegra was alive; the rest was nothing to me. More than likely, he had found some little-known historical fact about the image and simply wanted me to know – maybe as a distraction – but I waited nonetheless out of respect for him.

As the minutes passed, I glanced up at the large dome overhead, decorated with frescos and ornate gold trim. It always took me aback with its serene, awe-inspiring beauty, but I felt only impatience at this moment. Tapping my toe on the stone floor, I twisted my head to peer at the door, trying to will Father Gianni to appear. For the second time today, he kept me waiting and wondering . . .

When I could bear it no longer, I strolled toward the side altar door, expecting him to appear at any moment. When he did not, I let myself into the adjacent room known as the Old Sacristy, an ancient part of the basilica that allowed only priests. Once inside, I let my eyes adjust to the shadowed light and, as the room gradually became clear, I saw Father Gianni . . . lying crumpled beneath the marble statue of Cosimo de' Medici.

Quickly, I rushed forward to see if he was breathing, calling out for help: '*Aiuto! Aiuto!*' Kneeling down, I gently turned him over and saw a gaping wound near his heart.

Dio mio.

He had been stabbed and was bleeding profusely.

'*Aiuto! Aiuto!*'

Then the room began to spin into blackness.

Captain Parker's Log
April 8, 1815
At sea near Java

We have spent three days under full sail after leaving Makassar, attempting to find the source of the ash shower; it had continued to rain down on us since we first felt the explosion, but luckily we were able to navigate through it and catch enough wind to keep the Fortuna *moving southwest. Only a volcanic eruption could have caused the eerie darkness that blocked out the sun day and night and triggered the sooty taste in the air, but we had no sense of its origin.*

Any survivors would be in shock – starving and desperate – so we were compelled by a great sense of urgency.

At least the world had not ended.

First, we sailed to the village of Djokjakarta, on the island of Java, but found nothing amiss in the bustling streets when we went ashore – only people going about their business in the warm, stifling humidity. British authorities told me there might have been a small eruption from Mount Bromo on a mostly uninhabited part of the island to the east. They did not appear concerned since they had no reports of affected islanders, and the volcanic ash appeared to be falling less and less each day.

Still, we were unconvinced. The wildlife on Java seemed unnaturally hushed and still, as if waiting for nature to make its next move. Scant whiffs of an offshore breeze stirred the palm tree fronds and no birds appeared in the skies – a muted quiet that seemed to bode ill for the island.

We sailed the Fortuna *around the south shoreline of Java, scanning the mountain range with our telescopes for some sign of an active volcano: the jagged peaks of Merapi, Klut and Bromo could be seen in the distance, rugged yet calm. Their staggered formation dominated the landscape, but they, too, seemed quiet.*

Lowering my binoculars in puzzlement, I theorized

from the wind direction that the ash cloud must have drifted west from yet another island.

But which one?

I gazed up at the sun hidden behind thick, shaded skies as far as the eye could see, and rapidly calculated where the closest volcano was located.

Tambora. Due east, located on the northern shore of Sumbawa in the Java Sea, Mount Tambora had erupted many times in the distant past, but had lain dormant for the last century. Locals respected and feared its looming presence, but I had never actually seen it.

The Fire Mountain – that is what they called it.

When I told my men that we should set sail for Tambora, some of the Javanese exchanged glances of fear; I heard the words 'Mandara' and 'Saleh.' Not knowing what they meant, I asked my first mate to translate and, after some discussion with them, he told me that they spoke of a legendary kingdom, which once sat at the foot of Mount Tambora. Its ruler, King Mandara, had reportedly insulted a traveling merchant named Saleh who cursed him and caused the mountain to erupt and destroy the kingdom.

The Bay of Saleh was born.

I gave a dismissive shrug as he finished the story: a fairy tale. Even if it were true, that was long ago, and a thriving town now stood in its place.

But when my English crewmen heard the story, they crossed themselves and begged that we head back to Makassar until other British ships could join us; they also did not want to put our precious cargo at further risk.

For a few moments, I considered agreeing to their request, but then I shook off the foolishness of such thoughts. 'That is but a legend – a story told to entertain children,' I assured them. 'The eruption is over, and if it were Mount Tambora we need to make for the island to rescue any survivors. Following the rules of the sea, we cannot abandon them when it may be days before other vessels can join us. To be sure, our cargo will not suffer if we take a few more days to search.'

The men looked down, shuffling their feet on the deck in guilty assent.

So we sailed east, ever watchful for pirates who might also be drawn to the source of a natural disaster to pillage any unguarded villages.

We knew not what awaited us when we arrived at Tambora, but we were resolved.

The Fire Mountain.

FOUR

Villa Diodati, Geneva, Switzerland, 1816

'When will these storms end?' I moaned, staring out of the window. Sunless skies met the choppy waves of Lake Geneva in a tapestry of dreariness, day after day. The chilly winds. The endless cloudy days. The unrelenting lightning. 'You would think I had become used to this weather growing up in England, but I have never experienced such depressing weather.'

Mary sat next to the fireplace where the wood blazed its crackling warmth into the morning room – an intimate space, decorated with gilt furniture and a pink marble mantle; she was rocking William's cradle as she stared into the flames. 'It drains the spirit. I find myself drifting through the day like a ghost who is trying to find a restful place.'

'Maybe we *are* dead and simply do not know it,' I said, moving away from the window. Mary and I sat alone with little William in the room – Byron and Shelley had gone out riding in spite of the drizzle. Without their presence, we always found ourselves even more bored and restless with the gloomy weather. 'What do you think, Mary? Are we the living dead?'

She sighed. 'It feels like it – except that my sweet boy brings me back to the reality of being alive.' Smiling, she reached down and brushed his soft hair. 'Is he not the most beautiful creature that you have ever seen?'

'Of course.' I heard him make little baby noises that I now found so dear, considering my own condition. Surreptitiously, my hand covered the slight swell of my stomach hidden under my billowy white cotton dress.

A log broke apart in the fireplace, causing tiny embers to shoot up the chimney.

'Does he know about the child yet?' Mary asked.

I winced. 'No.'

As always, Mary surprised me with her perceptiveness. We had never spoken about my night-time visits with Byron, since I would wait until she and Shelley had retired for the evening before walking up the short path between our cottage and Diodati. But she knew me too well not to guess about my nocturnal activities.

'You will have to tell him soon . . .' Her face held a gentle warning. 'You don't want him to hear it from anyone else.'

'Polidori?'

She nodded. 'He does seem to make mischief wherever he goes and might drive a wedge between the two of you, if he could.'

I leaned my forehead against the mantle, staring down at the flames. 'He dislikes me intensely. I knew it from the first day that we met, but he feels quite differently about you—'

'Stop, Claire. I will not hear any of that nonsense.' Her translucent skin took on a flush that had nothing to do with her closeness to the fireplace. She was embarrassed because, much to everyone's surprise, Polidori had become enchanted with Mary. His eyes followed her everywhere, and he had recently taken to writing her the most desperate-sounding poetry. He was besotted and we were all quite amused by it – as much as I could apply humor to Byron's young physician.

Even as Polidori gazed longingly at Mary, I was the object of his sharp watchfulness. I could not prove that he had searched through my letters or broken my locket, but my suspicions remained unabated. He was my foe, though I remained puzzled as to why he had taken such a dislike to me from the moment that we met. Perhaps I had done him a wrong in another life. Perhaps he was jealous of my relationship with Byron – or Mary. Who knows? But I kept my distance and my own counsel on this matter. Byron would only laugh if I told him, and Shelley would plead with me to extend compassion to Polidori. Neither option seemed a likely choice for me. So I kept Mary as my sole confidante and stayed ever vigilant.

'When will you tell Byron about the child?' Mary pressed me.

'Soon.' I kept staring at the flames. 'I need to think about when it might be best to give him the news . . . when he is not so . . . bitter about having left his wife and his country. There is no question of marriage between us, of course. He has a wife, and I do not think she would want a divorce. Indeed, she is probably praying for his return.' Who would not want to be with him? 'No, my situation is very different. All I can really hope for is that he will love me and support our baby.'

'I do understand.' Mary's voice echoed through the room. 'Perhaps we were both too impetuous in our pursuit of love. Neither of them was free, but how could we not follow our hearts? Does not love truly trump all social convention? All mundane definitions of morality?'

Glancing over my shoulder, I shot her a glance of irony. 'Are you trying to convince me or yourself?'

She sighed. 'Both, I suppose.'

I moved back to the settee and sat next to Mary, looking down at William's face – so sweet in repose. 'What is done is done now. We can never go back. And would we, even if we had the chance? You would not have William, and I would not be expecting my own child. No, this is our destiny, and we must embrace it.'

'Why, Claire, you sound so different from when we first left England – almost fatalistic.'

'Perhaps copying out Byron's new canto of *Childe Harold* has affected me,' I admitted. 'Every line is about loss and the endless cycles of change in history – some of the verses moved me to tears yesterday. "For pleasures past I do not grieve, / Nor perils gathering near; / My greatest grief is that I leave / No thing that claims a tear." Is that not the most tragic thing that no one would mourn our deaths?'

'Do not dwell on such dark thoughts,' Mary warned, gently squeezing my shoulders. 'It can do no good for you or the child – trust me. Besides, you will always have my support; do not doubt that.'

Truly?

I leaned my head on her shoulder as we did when young girls. Although I was the more headstrong of the two of us,

I relied on Mary's strength of character and purpose. Often, I felt drawn in many directions, pulled by the whims of the moment, but Mary grounded me and brought me back to reality.

'Remember when your father, Godwin, married my mother and brought my brother, Charles, and me into your household? I was terrified that he would change his mind and send Mama and us back to the tiny, cramped rooms in south London,' I reminisced as she smoothed down my wild curls. 'You took my hand the first day . . .'

'And showed you all of my books, from Milton's *Paradise Lost* to Defoe's *Robinson Crusoe*,' she finished for me with a soft voice. 'Could anything have been more tedious than going through every title on my bookshelf?'

'I found it quite kind, though I was never as single-minded about learning as you.'

'True – and I did not have your ear for languages.'

'*C'est vrai.*'

Mary laughed. 'I never thought anything would come between us as sisters – and it has not.' *Yet.* The word was left unspoken.

'But men sometimes have a way of changing the bonds between women.' I raised my head and met her eyes, directly and honestly. 'We are never so vulnerable as when we are in love. I was so happy for you and Shelley when you pledged your eternal devotion to each other at your mama's grave. She would have been pleased, but I wanted to have a great love myself.' I had helped Mary in her secret assignations with Shelley in the cemetery where her mother, the great writer, Mary Wollstonecraft, was buried – and paid the price of my own mother's disapproval when she found out. Yet I was willing to brave her displeasure in the cause of true love.

Mary's eyes shuttered down, and I knew why; she often found the heritage of a famous mother a difficult weight to bear.

'Byron cares for me – in his own way.' I tried to sound confident, but my voice seemed uncertain, even to my own ears. I had been so eager to see him, to take up where we left off with our passionate encounters outside London. But during the last few weeks, even though I loved him more than ever, *he* was a changed man from the fiercely ardent poet who became my lover in England. Sad. Bitter. Lonely.

When we all huddled around the fire at Diodati, conversing on his favorite topics, which ranged from Aristotle's *Poetics* to his exploits in Albania as a young man, Byron's enthusiasm held a hollow note. We had given him the nickname Albe, much to his amusement. But love? I could not say.

Mary coughed lightly. 'He is a lost soul, and I am not sure he can love with anything but half a heart. In spite of his bravado, I can see that our dear Albe still mourns the loss of his old life: the social whirl in London and the literati that worshipped him. It is all gone now. I suppose we do not really understand what he has given up since we have never had that kind of fame and adoration, but I think we are poor substitutes.'

I exhaled with a whisper of sad agreement.

'But his affections *are* engaged with you, Claire – I know it. And he is not the type of man who would abandon his responsibilities to his own child, no matter what occurs between the two of you.' She must have felt the sudden squeeze of pain in my heart because her tone took on a much lighter aspect. 'At any rate, we are happy enough here in our magic circle, so it may all work out in the way that you hope, once he has had time to adjust to his new life.'

'Yes. I believe that may be so,' I responded quickly, grasping at the sweet possibility of happiness with every fiber of my being; I would do anything to make it happen. 'There are certainly no two poets who find each other's company more congenial, or who love sailing more. This is an almost perfect place for those two occupations.'

'If only Shelley would remember to feed the chicken,' Mary moaned theatrically and we both laughed, breaking the sudden blanket of melancholy that had descended over us. We had bought the chicken, whom we named Gertie, to provide fresh eggs for William, but Shelley constantly forgot to feed her and she had grown alarmingly thin. Needless to say, Gertie's egg production had declined as well. 'I know great men must think great thoughts, but perhaps they could also—'

'Feed the chicken?' I raised my brows, imitating Byron's habitually sardonic expression. 'I think not.'

We laughed again.

Just then, the large oak door swung open and Polidori hobbled in, causing our happy mood to dim. He had been trying to impress Mary a few days ago by jumping over a fence; unfortunately, he had landed on a rabbit hole. He'd sprained his left foot and consequently endured endless mockery from Byron, who termed him 'the Knight Gallant.' Of course, his injury prevented him from joining in Shelley and Byron's ramblings, providing him cause to remain with us as he recovered.

A most unhappy outcome for Mary and me.

'How are you feeling?' Mary inquired politely, extending her hand towards him.

'Somewhat better.' He made an elaborate bow as he clasped her palm, but when he attempted to raise her fingers to his lips, she pulled back.

'I am very glad to hear that.' She cleared her throat awkwardly.

He turned in my direction. 'Miss Claire.'

'Dr Polidori.'

We acknowledged each other as fighters moving into a ring, readying themselves for a bare-knuckle battle. I did not welcome our usual clash of wills, but I would not back down either in the face of his distaste.

Admittedly handsome, Polidori was barely a few years older than Mary and me, but he possessed an air of one who thought a great deal of himself, as if he had achieved a degree of success equal to that of his employer. He displayed the arrogance of an ambitious man, ever watchful of an opportunity to push himself forward.

Personally, I did not understand why Byron even tolerated him.

Now that he had become attached to Mary, I found Shelley's patience with him even more disconcerting.

'We expect Byron and Shelley shortly; they took the sailboat across the lake to Geneva this morning to see the old cathedral at Yvoire,' I said, stressing the imminence of their arrival and hoping that he would not linger.

Polidori seated himself, stretching out his injured leg.

Drat the man.

'I hear that you are copying one of Byron's new cantos of *Childe Harold*,' he began with a smile – a sly twist of his mouth that hardly reached his eyes. 'That must be very . . . enlightening for you.'

'And your meaning, sir?' I responded, my eyes narrowing.

Polidori flicked an imaginary speck of lint from his dark jacket. 'Only that you probably find it moving to see the words of the great poet himself before anyone else's eyes read the lines. You are his muse – his editor perhaps? Indeed, I imagine that your hand probably trembles as you write . . .'

I clenched my jaw, knowing he was baiting me. But I, too, could play that game.

'Yes, it does.' Smiling sweetly, I continued, 'Being in the presence of *true* brilliance can be daunting, but I find it brings out only the best in me – as opposed to others who are consumed with petty jealousy at the thought of their lesser talent.' I stressed the last two words delicately.

Mary stifled a giggle.

He frowned. 'I assume you reference me, Miss Claire?'

'Indeed, no – I had no one in particular in mind. It is just a general comment.' I rose and moved towards the fire, reaching for a log. But before I could toss it into the flames, Polidori was at my side and took the piece of wood from me.

'You should let men attend the fire – it is hardly the job of women.' He threw it into the hearth, causing deep, red flames to rise upwards in fiery spikes. A tiny spark shot out and singed my arm. I winced.

'Are you all right?' Mary exclaimed.

'I am fine.'

Polidori seized my arm and rubbed his thumb over the small, reddish spot. 'You see, Miss Claire? When you play with fire, you can get burned.'

Snatching my arm out of his grasp, I stepped back. 'I have a thick skin and can take care of myself.' But the sharp pain had caused tears to sting at my eyes. I turned away so he could not see my face, but he could probably sense that I was lying. Why did he provoke me so?

'Perhaps I misjudged you,' he said from behind me. 'If so, you are a formidable woman.'

In truth, I was *not* that type of female; I was, in fact, quite vulnerable – unmarried with a child on the way. Polidori's very presence seemed a threat to me because I did not understand his insinuations as he hovered around us like a malevolent spirit, planting doubt and uncertainty.

Massaging my arm, I kept my back to him as I seated myself again next to Mary.

'Do not let him annoy you so, Claire; he is only trying to prove he is your superior,' she whispered, 'which he is *not*.'

I gave a little shake of my head but did not respond. It was more than provocation; it was malice, pure and simple. But Mary did not truly see that in him. She viewed Polidori as the silly young man who constantly tried to impress her and whom she held at arm's length, secure in Shelley's love.

Polidori flung himself into a chair opposite us and stared into the fire in silence for a short time. Then he finally spoke up. 'I wonder how all of those people who died in that volcano eruption last year felt as they drew their last breath. Did they know they were going to die? Did they suffer long?'

Mary moved her hand to her mouth briefly, her eyes widening in dismay. 'What are you talking about?'

He swung his face in her direction. 'I was reading about that volcano that exploded in the Far East last summer – Mount Tambora. It buried whole villages in a matter of minutes, so the residents could not outrun the heat and lava flow. Imagine that? In the blink of an eye—'

'Dear God, Polidori!' Mary interjected. 'What evil sprite has taken possession of you to talk about such things?'

'Life and death?' He gave a mocking laugh. 'That is my profession, my dear Mary. I am a physician, after all.'

She stiffened, her face turning pale and cold. 'I would ask that you do not address me with such familiarity, sir.'

'I stand corrected, Mrs Shelley, and I apologize.' His tone sounded anything but apologetic.

Most locals referred to Mary with the title of a married woman but, in truth, everyone knew she and Shelley were not wed.

'Accepted.' She sat back, somewhat mollified. But I was not convinced that he had the least bit of regret for his over-familiarity. Nor had I heard him talk like that whenever Byron and Shelley were present. No, his presuming ways were confined to Mary and me when we had no male protectors present. Cowardly and rude.

'You must admit that the thought of a volcano on the other side of the world creating such massive destruction is compelling,' he continued, 'causing us to live in perpetual darkness here in Geneva with the rain and clouds.'

'I have nothing but sympathy for those who died or may have known someone who died,' I chimed in, looking down at little William with a shudder. 'It would cut out a woman's heart to lose a husband or a child.'

'So true.' Mary clutched the cradle in a protective gesture. 'To lose a loved one is torture to the soul, a pain that can cause the most resilient person to behave rashly, even to the point of wanting to cut through the veil that separates life from death.'

'Bringing the dead back?' Polidori queried. 'Do you think that is possible?'

'No,' I blurted out.

'Yes,' Mary said simultaneously.

He folded his arms across his chest, smiling. 'So the sisters finally disagree on something? Who would have thought that was possible, or that it would be on the subject of resurrection?'

I started to protest, but Mary held up a hand and proceeded to answer for us. 'I am not saying we can play God and animate the dead – *now*. I agree with Claire. But in the future, who knows? Science may be showing us the way through . . . electricity.'

'*Brava*.' Polidori clapped his hands. 'Very diplomatic, if unrealistic.'

'Even if we *could* bring back those whom we have lost, it is not something mankind *should* attempt,' I cut in. 'The departed have left us, never to return. That is the way of nature, and we must respect it.'

'You will feel differently, Claire, when you become a

mother,' Mary said, lifting William on to her lap with a soft kiss against his cheek.

'You will, indeed,' Polidori added under his breath before he exited.

Mary did not hear him, but I did.

He knew my secret.

'Let us all tell a ghost story,' Byron said that night after dinner as our little group convened in the huge parlor of the Villa Diodati – sans Polidori, who had a dinner engagement in Geneva. He would *not* be missed by me. The evening chill had crept in with its foggy dampness, so we huddled close to the immense fireplace. Byron stood near the window, staring out at the darkness relieved only by flashes of jagged lightning. 'And as we each recite some tale of terror, we will see who is the first one of us who flees in fright—'

'Oh, yes – but let me set the stage first with my new poem,' Shelley said as he began to pace around the room, reciting lines from his new lyric. 'I need a distraction from this "Hymn to Intellectual Beauty" – it simply will not allow me to write it.' He flipped the notebook shut and collapsed on to the settee next to my stepsister. 'Perhaps you should write it for me, Mary.'

'I would not presume to try poetry. No, that is your forte.' She stroked the back of his neck in a tender gesture that was usually reserved for William, who was sleeping quietly back at the cottage, watched over by a village girl. 'The lines will come to you, never fear.'

'But I do fear that I will never find the words again. Maybe I have already written all that I have inside me.' Shelley raked a hand through his hair, causing it to stand up in wild disarray. Much as he loved roaming the area on horseback with Byron, he always returned in an agitated state, almost as if nature fed a wellspring that threatened to drown his skill to write about it. I also suspected that Byron's brilliance tended to eclipse Shelley's confidence.

Byron, of course, had the opposite reaction: he would turn very genial and prolific, often composing dozens of verses in a single evening, and he became more affectionate to those around him. I took what he had to offer at those times.

'Perhaps my Muse has died.' Shelley dropped his head with a moan of despair.

I began to protest from my seat across from them, but Byron chimed in first: 'Nonsense. There is no better poet in Europe than you, my friend. And the world will soon discover that once my publisher, Murray, puts out a new edition of your poetry. You will find the fame you seek.'

'And who would know better than Albe?' Mary tossed a smile of gratitude at Byron.

He bowed and began singing one of his favorite Albanian folk songs in a loud voice that rang out across the room, slightly off key. None of us knew the lyrics, but his stylized performance caused laughter to bubble up, shifting the atmosphere away from Shelley's poetic demons.

Once Byron had finished, he moved to his mahogany wine caddy and poured himself a glass of Madeira, downing almost the entire contents in one gulp. Then he refilled his glass and strolled over to our side of the room, dragging his clubfoot rather more heavily than usual. 'I learned that song during my Grand Tour stop with the Ali Pasha – known as a despot and a rogue, but his hospitality was second to none.'

'Was he the model for Pasha Seyd in *The Corsair*?' I queried, hoping to distract him from drinking huge quantities of wine; it did not take long for him to shift into acerbity and bitter quips.

'Partially, though I found him more fatherly than fearsome in my youth.' He stood behind me and I felt his warm breath against the bare skin of my back, causing an instant wave of desire. Mary and I always wore our best (and only) silk frocks for an evening at the villa. We possessed few dresses, but dinner demanded some semblance of fashion, even in such an isolated setting. So we would don our pastel-colored frocks, with the low-cut empire necklines and billowy skirts that suited both of us, especially me with my generous curves and petite figure. The poets might dominate our conversation with their brilliance, but we wove a sensual thread through the tapestry of our evenings by always appearing to our advantage.

Poetry and passion. An irresistible combination.

'You certainly have a fondness for the country of Albania,' Mary interjected.

'It was actually quite a miserable place – horrible roads and endless heat during the summer – but the beauty of the women was unparalleled.' More breaths against my neck, tinged with alcohol.

My heartbeat increased to a rapid staccato as he circled my chair, trailing his fingers across my throat. I was his prey, wanting to be caught.

'Some say Claire herself looks quite Mediterranean,' Shelley said as his eyes did an inventory of my features. I felt the heat rise to my face, but I was pleased to be the center of attention in our little circle – for once. 'Dark eyes, dusky skin, jet-black curls . . . just like the Ali Pasha's daughter, protected from the world in a harem until love awakens her deepest longings—'

'You seem to have found your poetic voice again,' Mary cut in, her tone now sharp. Ever watchful that Shelley might show me too much fondness, she had little patience when his flights of fancy extended to me.

'Inspired, no doubt, by the beauty around us.' Byron raised his glass to Mary and me; the awkward moment passed like the flare of a candle in the wind. But it was there between us – always there.

A crack of thunder split through the silence, causing me to jump and then glance at the window nervously. 'The storms seem worse this evening now the wind has picked up; it feels as if we are in the midst of a tempest . . .'

'A perfect night to tell ghost stories,' Byron continued as he took a seat, completing our circle. The magic seemed to intertwine around us, charging the very air with creative energy. 'Shall I begin?'

'Please do,' I urged.

'It is not a story, but a poem that I have been working on.' He leaned his head back against the headrest and toyed with his wine glass as he began to recite in a low voice: "I had a dream, which was not all a dream. / The bright sun was extinguish'd, and the stars / Did wander darkling in the eternal

space, / Rayless, and pathless, and the icy earth / Swung blind
and blackening in the moonless air . . ."'

Mary gave an anxious little cough, and the color drained
from her already pale face. 'I have had that identical dream
where I wandered the earth as the last person left after a
cataclysm – it was a dark and empty world without friends or
family. One without hope,' she said in a hushed tone and
visibly shuddered. 'I cannot imagine a worse fate than to be
all alone . . . forever.'

He nodded slowly, solemnly. 'I call the poem "Darkness."'

Now, it was my turn to shiver. Was that to be our future?
Dreadful solitude and loneliness permeating our last days?

Surely fate could not be that unkind.

Another crack of thunder rumbled outside – louder and
stronger – causing the shutters to rattle.

Before I lost my nerve, I spoke up. 'I have a ghost story in
mind of a woman who is so independent of character and
mind that her lover rejects her. She then dies and haunts him
forever . . . I titled it "The Idiot."'

'It sounds like Annabella, my wife.' Byron gave a bitter
guffaw. 'For my part, I want no more of that type of woman
– she certainly made our life together idiotic at best, tragic at
worst.'

A tense silence enveloped the room; no one responded.

'Surely not *all* was bad,' Shelley finally spoke up. 'You
have a daughter, and she is part of you, no matter what. You
must remember that always.'

Byron turned his head slowly and looked at Shelley as
though he were a visitor from another world – an alien place
far away from his own jaded perspective. 'You are one of the
best men that I have known in my life, and I am not worthy
of your friendship. Perhaps if the world had treated me better,
I would have the finer qualities of a gentleman such as you,
Shelley.'

Shelley simply smiled. 'I, too, have my faults – as Mary
can tell you.'

Shaking her head slightly, she responded, 'My only protest
is that you become so consumed in your poetry and reading
that you forget to eat.'

Byron laughed again, but the bitterness had lightened somewhat.

'Claire, you must write your story of "The Idiot,"' Shelley enthused, 'and promise to scare us down to our bones when you read it.'

'I agree.' Byron flashed a glance of mild interest in my direction. 'It will certainly . . . entertain us.'

A glow of delight flowed through me. In truth, I had been writing the novel since we first came to Geneva, but I did not have the courage to share it with anyone yet. Growing up in my family, one had to possess the skill to write great epics or be consigned into the oblivion of a lesser being. I would make my ghost story place myself in the first group.

Shelley beamed, which caused Mary to frown again.

'I want to join in the competition,' Polidori said in a slurred voice as he ambled into the room, with only a slight limp from his injured ankle and an unsteady gait, probably from opium or alcohol. His face looked flushed, his eyes wild. I instantly stiffened in discomfort.

'Polidori, have you been taking too much laudanum again?' Byron asked.

'Perhaps.' He snickered and narrowed his eyes. 'Did you want it for yourself, my lord?'

Mary and I exchanged glances of alarm, waiting for Byron to explode in a tirade against his tedious young doctor.

Surprisingly, Byron tilted back his head and stared at the ceiling with a groan of impatience. 'Don't be a bore, Polidori. If I wanted laudanum, I would simply take it from you. By all means, join the competition, but you had better write something beyond the drivel that you have already shown to me. Better yet, I will give you a story and you can expand on it for us – as long as you promise to make our blood run cold.'

'I promise.' Polidori held up his hand as if taking a solemn oath.

I choked back a cry of protest. *Do not encourage him.*

'An excellent idea,' Shelley enthused. 'And now we have to hear only from Mary. Will you write a ghostly narrative to terrify one and all, my love?'

All eyes riveted on Mary – especially Polidori's. He stood next to her, swaying slightly like a sailor on a pitching deck.

'I . . . I have nothing in mind at the moment, but I will try to write something.' She reached out to Shelley, threading her fingers through his. 'Though I cannot believe that my words could strike terror into any reader—'

'Fear assumes many disguises,' Polidori interjected with a note of sarcasm. 'I am unnerved by *everything* that you say, and I would be a happy man if you tried to terrify me . . .' As he leaned towards Mary, he lost his balance and began to fall on her. But I instantly rose and shoved him to the side, causing him to tumble on to the floor with a hard thud. He shouted in pain, and we all rushed to his side as he clutched his boot, except for Byron, who merely shook his head, muttering, 'Foolish boy.'

Shelley knelt down and gently lifted Polidori's leg, turning it to one side and then the other.

Polidori whimpered.

'We had better take him to his room and put a poultice on the sprain,' Shelley suggested as he helped Polidori to his feet. Then he shifted the young doctor's arm around his own thin shoulders and walked him out of the room, followed by Mary.

When they had exited, I confronted Byron. 'Why do you encourage him? He is rude, obnoxious and childish. He is supposed to be your doctor, but he spends his days consumed with drink and opium and constantly provokes Mary with his disrespectful overtures. He cannot be allowed to continue with this appalling behavior.'

Byron averted his head and drained the last of his wine. 'I shall speak to him.'

'Thank you.' I touched his cheek and he flinched.

Turning away from him, my heart squeezed in disappointment. 'Why will you not let me love you? I do, you know. More than I can say. Yet you seem only to trifle with me as if I were but a meaningless speck of dust in your life. I thought things would be different in Geneva, but it seems that I was wrong. You want me, but you do not want to be *with* me.'

He sighed deeply. 'I made no vow, no pledge beyond what

I could give to you, Claire. I have no such feelings anymore. That part of me is dead – as dead as the withered branches of a lifeless tree. I wish I could have your optimism and passion for life, but that time is over for me. I am not the man I was . . .'

'It does not have to be like that.' I struggled to keep myself composed, but it was all that I could do not to blurt out that new life stirred inside of me. 'Does it?'

'Perhaps . . . not.'

Was there a flicker of hope in his tone?

'I know we can never marry since you still have a wife, but I could make you happy.' I bit my lip, trying to find the right words that might inspire him to find faith in the future. Our future. 'You have enjoyed our time in Geneva, have you not? You get on well with Shelley and Mary? We could remain here or go to Italy – wherever, as long as we are together. The four of us . . . our charmed circle.' Without Polidori.

I heard him take in a sharp breath, but he said nothing.

A heaviness came over me at his mute response. It was pointless to keep trying to resurrect the man that I had once known; he was gone forever. With a deep sigh, I began to move away, but he seized my hand.

'No – wait.'

I paused and turned slowly.

'Do not leave me.' His eyes melted into my soul, full of entreaty and desire. 'I cannot be alone with my thoughts – they are haunting me tonight. The ghosts of my past. Images of people whom I have wronged . . . I did not mean to hurt any of them, least of all you, Claire.'

The rain began to fall outside in a hard, loud torrent, beating against the windows.

Slipping my arms around his shoulders, I held him tightly in a fierce embrace. 'I knew the risks.' Except to my heart. I never thought he would break my heart. 'It was my choice.'

He sought my lips, his kiss punishing and angry, almost as if I had to be chastised for giving in to him. I would be hurt yet again, perhaps even more deeply – I knew it. He would never love me . . . but I could live in the moment, for now, and forget about the consequences. It would all crash down in the end, and I would pay dearly for my indiscretion, but tonight was ours.

A week later, the storms had abated somewhat, so we decided to embrace the day and lounge under the striped awning at the villa overlooking the lake. By late afternoon, the sun peeped out just before it began to drop below the horizon, a sliver of red and gold stretching across the lower sky in jagged streaks of color and light.

Shelley lounged on a chaise, reading an excerpt of Rousseau's novel *Julie* to Mary and me: 'Listen to this passage: "Virtue is a state of war, and to live in it means one always has some battle to wage against oneself." So poetic and so true. Rousseau never avoided the truth, however painful. We all do battle with ourselves.'

'But does that not give us even more appreciation of the victories?' I countered from my perch on the top step where I sat, hugging my knees to my chest.

'For some – and for others it leads to melancholy self-doubt,' Mary agreed as she finished her latest sketch of the lake, shading in the pine trees that dotted the coastline. She had been trying to perfect her drawing skills as a distraction from not being able to pen a ghost story. Shelley and I had spent much of the week babbling away about our own gothic tales, but she took no part in the conversations, just drifted around the cottage with a distracted expression.

'Rousseau teaches us that love is the way to counter this sad reality,' he posed, resting the open book on his leg. 'That is the one virtue in the world: to always follow the truth of our feelings, no matter where it leads us.'

'And you speak from experience?' I teased.

'Indeed, yes.' He snapped the book shut with a short chuckle. 'I am a soldier of many campaigns on the field of love.'

Acknowledging his witticism, I inclined my head. 'And to the victor go the spoils.'

'Claire, do not encourage him in this talk,' Mary warned as she took one last critical scan of her sketch, adding a few strokes near the edges of the paper. 'It is foolish.'

'You are most unkind, my dear.' He gazed at the clear blue

color of the water reflecting the shimmering rays of the waning sun. 'I have half a mind to propose that Byron and I play the tourist and take the boat to every spot where Rousseau set a scene in *Julie* – from the castle at Chillon to Vevey. Indeed, we can take our own literary pilgrimage.'

Mary sighed. 'Men only, I presume?'

'Do you really want to take a boat trip with Albe and . . . his quirks?' he whispered.

We did not respond, knowing Byron's maddening travel eccentricities only too well, from his odd sleeping habits to the enormous amount of luggage he transported. It would no doubt require a great deal of patience (and courage) to embark on an expedition with him. Much as I found his presence unbearably exciting, I preferred being with him on *terra firma*.

'You two must go – alone,' Mary hastened to add.

'Go where?' Byron emerged from inside the villa, Polidori in tow, along with another man whom I had not met. Slightly older than Polidori, the newcomer was of medium stature, with classically Italian features and somewhat romantic attire: open-collared shirt and breeches. He held back until Byron introduced him. 'This is Ludovico di Breme, recently arrived from Italy. I met him at Madame de Stael's yesterday and persuaded him to come by.'

'*Buongiorno,*' he murmured as he bowed to us.

Mary and I murmured polite greetings. We did not attend de Stael's *salon* gatherings that attracted many of the local expatriates. The middle-aged, French aristocratic exile pretended to espouse social liberalism and revolutionary politics, but she disapproved of Mary and me, and our open living arrangements with married men. Byron, of course, suffered none of this condemnation – he was too famous, too handsome.

Shelley stood and shook hands with di Breme, then they immediately drew off to the side and began talking about Italian politics. Mary resumed her sketching as I pretended to contemplate the lake's translucent surface, though I listened intently to snatches of their discussion, catching words like '*carbonari*' and '*Risorgimento.*'

Who was this di Breme? An Italian revolutionary?

All of a sudden, I felt him studying me with a secret, sidelong glance. Shifting uncomfortably, I pretended not to notice and engaged Mary in some talk about William's teething problems, but I sensed his regard continued.

I picked up Shelley's book and tried to focus on Rousseau's novel.

'Signorina Clairmont?' I heard him say as he reached out his hand. 'The stone steps must be growing cold. May I assist you to stand?'

Looking up, I gave him a polite smile. Then, as he helped me to my feet, I noted that an odd expression flitted over his face akin to . . . curiosity. My mouth tightened. He must have heard gossip about us at de Stael's. I hated that. It made me feel like some type of trapped, exotic animal in a circus.

Mentally shrugging off my reaction, I welcomed him in Italian, which instantly caused his face to brighten as he shifted into his native language and explained that he was spending the summer in nearby Coppet to escape the Mediterranean heat.

'You certainly have come to the right place to avoid the sultry Italian climate,' I pointed out. 'It has been decidedly cool in Geneva.' We continued the pleasantries for a few minutes in Italian, and I found myself gradually warming to his open, frank manners, even as he warmed to mine.

'Claire, do not monopolize our guest,' Byron said in a sharp tone. 'Especially when he was just about to leave.'

'Are you not staying to dinner?' I queried, now in English.

He took a brief, backward glimpse at Byron, then said in Italian, 'I am afraid that I cannot stay, but perhaps we can chat another time?'

'*Si.*' I extended my hand to him. 'I would like that.'

He disappeared into the villa with Byron, and I never saw him again.

It was only much later that evening, when we had all taken refuge indoors again, that Mary asked about di Breme.

Byron was eagerly surveying a map with Shelley for their proposed sailing trip and did not glance up. 'Madame de Stael gave him letters of introduction to me. A pleasing-enough young man who, by her account, was once an abbé and, then, abandoned religion for literature; she thought I might offer him some advice about his poetry.'

'And did you?' I prompted, more puzzled than ever about our recent guest.

'It is hardly worth my time to contemplate since I daresay I shall not encounter him again,' Byron commented absently, then focused on the map once more. 'Shelley, we must see the Château de Chillon; it is at the farthest northern point of the lake and, from what I have heard, quite magnificent – if you like old ruins.'

'I have heard the castle once housed François Bonivard – a political prisoner who was chained to a pillar in one of the lower levels for seven long years.' Mary stood behind them, peering over Shelley's shoulder. 'You must sketch the dungeon for me.'

'How could a man endure that type of imprisonment for so long?' Byron touched the spot on the map where it said Chillon. 'I would have gone mad.'

'Anyone would have lost his sanity,' Polidori echoed. He seemed to be interested in their trip, but I could tell from the straight, tight line of his lips that he was annoyed not to be invited to join them.

'Perhaps it is just a legend,' Shelley said, 'but we must stop there and see for ourselves. And I want see "Julie's bower" at Clarens, where she and her lover shared their first kiss in the novel. To tread that ground would be a tribute to Rousseau and all of those who find their soulmate in this harsh reality of ours.'

'Indeed, yes,' Byron agreed.

After another hour, they had their route planned, and we celebrated over a glass of wine with our spirits high – even Polidori, who seemed quite congenial.

Not long afterwards, the thunderstorms rolled in and we were yet again subjected to the most violent rain and wind which set my nerves on edge as the lightning flashed in the windows with explosive intensity. Blindingly bright. Illuminating the room in a weird, distorted glow. Shelley's face grew more and more agitated with each separate flare, causing us to cluster near the fireplace around him. Once the thunder abated somewhat, he calmed down.

'Perhaps we should read our ghost stories now,' Byron proposed as he refilled his glass. 'It seems fitting that we voyage to strange new lands of the imagination on the eve of our actual voyage around the lake.'

'I have not finished my tale,' Shelley chimed in, 'but Mary told me this morning that she finally had an idea for her story—'

'No, it was just a fragment,' she protested.

'We *must* hear it,' Polidori exclaimed.

With a quick appeal for reassurance to Shelley and me, Mary cleared her throat. 'When I went to sleep a fortnight ago, I had a waking dream and saw a student kneeling beside the form of a creature he had pieced together from various body parts stolen from dead bodies that he had dug up. A hideous phantasm of a man. Then the student worked on a . . . machine that produced electricity and jolted the creature into showing signs of life. He stirred with an uneasy, half-vital motion . . . and was *alive*.'

A loud clap of thunder exploded outside.

I dropped my glass and it shattered on the stone floor. Then Shelley began to scream, pointing at Mary, exclaiming that he saw spirits rising from her chest. He dashed out of the room – still shrieking in a high-pitched tone that reverberated throughout the thick walls of the villa. Calling out his name, Mary hastened after him, along with Byron.

I began to follow them, but Polidori quickly moved to block my exit.

'Please stand aside – I need to attend to Shelley,' I said in a firm voice, but he did not alter his stance.

'By all means, but you should know that I have guessed your secret.' His face drew in close to mine. 'You think to tie Byron to you with his child, but it will only push him away. If I were you, I would rid myself of the burden.' He paused. 'Just say the word, and I will provide you with the medical means to do it.'

'Never.'

'You see me as your enemy, but I am not.' His eyes captured mine and, for a brief moment, I almost believed him. Then I shoved past him and stumbled out of the room.

As I reached the front entrance hall, I did not know where to turn next.

Miss Eliza's Weekly Fashion and Gossip Pamphlet
June 10, 1816, Geneva

The Ladies' Page
I promised to give all of you an update on the new beau monde *residents at the Villa Diodati, and here it is, dear readers.*
The rumors are true!
Lord Byron is presently living at Diodati and has befriended fellow British poet, Percy Bysshe Shelley. The two gentlemen have been spied taking horseback rides through the countryside of Cologny, and they are now rumored to be on an extended sailing trip around Lake Geneva. (Too bad for the curious who have hoped for a glimpse of the handsome young aristocrats.)
But who are the two young ladies with our fair poets? After some detective work, yours truly has learned their identities: Miss Mary Godwin and her stepsister, Miss Claire Clairmont – both recently from the London home of their father, William Godwin, noted writer and anarchist. Miss Godwin is also rumored to have a child with her, and there is some speculation that the father is none other than Shelley himself.
Could it be true?
Remember, ladies, Miss Godwin is also the daughter of Mary Wollstonecraft – an avowed advocate of free love – so it is entirely possible that she is following her mother's scandalous views. I shall have more news on this tittle-tattle soon . . .
Miss Clairmont is traveling as Miss Godwin's companion.

FIVE

Florence, Italy, 1873

'Aunt Claire, can you hear me? Are you all right?' A disembodied voice drifted through the fog of my own mind and it sounded familiar. As my eyelids fluttered open, I saw the anxious faces of Paula and Raphael hovering above me and, gradually, I became aware that my niece was stroking my forehead with a damp cloth.

'I . . . I think so.' Struggling to focus on my surroundings, I noted the familiar crooked crystal chandelier hanging from the frescoed ceiling of my bedroom. I exhaled in relief. *Home. In all of its shabby splendor.*

She dipped the cloth in a bowl of water, wrung it out and placed it over my forehead. 'You fainted at the Basilica di San Lorenzo . . . Do you remember what happened?'

My eyes widened as the memories came flooding back.

Father Gianni. He was dead.

I gasped as the memories of finding his dead body came rushing back. The pool of blood flaring out like deep red wings of fire around him. His twisted, broken body at the foot of Cosimo de' Medici's statue. His eyes flung open with that unstaring, vacant look of death. I crossed myself, murmuring a quick prayer for my lost, dear friend.

Paula kept her hand on the cloth. 'When you did not come out of the basilica, the driver went in to look for you—'

'And found me in the Old Sacristy with Father Gianni,' I finished for her in a grim tone. 'I can scarcely believe it, though I saw him with my own eyes.'

'Apparently, he was . . . stabbed,' Paula said with a shudder. Raphael slipped an arm around her waist, and she leaned in closer to him. 'After he found you, the driver shouted for the *polizia*. Then an unknown man helped to carry you outside to the carriage, and the driver ferried you back here.'

As she narrated the events, I had a vague recollection of several priests hovering around me at the basilica and, after that, the sensation of floating out to the carriage. 'I seem to recall someone who cradled me in a comforting embrace on the trip home – a savior. Did you see who brought me home with the driver?'

'No. You were alone in the carriage when Raphael and I came down for you,' she responded.

Frowning in concentration, I tried to summon clearer images of the sequence of events. 'But *someone* drove back with me.'

'The driver would know,' Raphael pointed out. 'I will question him.'

'Aunt Claire, what is going on?' Paula removed the damp cloth and held it in a tight grip as she locked glances with me. 'You did not visit Father Gianni to confess, did you? The Old Sacristy is far from the confessionals at the basilica.'

Holding her worried gaze for a few moments, I realized that I could not lie to her any longer. Paula was too dear to me, and she deserved to hear the truth. Forcing myself to sit up, I took in a deep breath and launched into my story. 'I went to see him yesterday because I was distraught and needed my old friend's counsel.'

'Because of Mr Rossetti's visit?' she queried.

Nodding, I reached under my pillow and retrieved the note about Allegra. As I handed it to Paula, I explained how I had found it under my teacup the previous day.

She scanned it quickly. 'I . . . I do not understand. I thought your daughter died when she was quite young.'

'Yes, of typhus – or so I thought all these years.' Taking back the note, I read the words again: *Your daughter lives.*

I bit my lip to keep it from trembling.

Paula shook her head. 'How is it possible that this fact could have been hidden from you for so long? You would have had some inkling, some bit of suspicion that she was still alive.'

Folding the note again, I clasped Paula's hand. 'I always had a doubt about her fate since I never actually saw her body; it was conveyed to England and buried near the church at Harrow. At the time, I received only a letter and death certificate from the Convent of Bagnacavallo, both of which have been lost over time. That is why I asked to meet Father Gianni yesterday. I told him everything, and he was researching the convent's death records that are housed in the Medici Library at San Lorenzo. In truth, he had little hope that Allegra had survived, though he contacted the present Mother Superior at the convent.' My heart squeezed in secret optimism. 'But I wanted to know – no matter what. That is why I went to see him this morning: to see what he had found out.'

'And he ended up dead,' Raphael said as he tightened his arm around Paula protectively.

I started to fill them in on the rest of the details when I realized that one of our family was missing. 'Where is Georgiana?'

'Do not worry, Aunt. After Raphael brought you in, I left her with her friend, Maria, and her family so you would not be disturbed,' Paula reassured me. 'Now, tell us everything that happened at the basilica.'

I closed my eyes briefly to compose myself and then began, 'Father Gianni was supposed to meet me at the high altar in the Medici Chapel, but he was late, very late. So I waited. When he finally appeared in some agitation, he said that he had begun to research Allegra's supposed death at the convent, though he had scant hope that she had survived. After that, he disappeared into the Sacristy for some document. He did not return, so I went to seek him, thinking he must have been detained.' The image of his crumpled body rose in my mind again, and I felt the tears run down my cheeks. 'It was terrible. A violent death. I can only hope that his final moments came quickly and that he did not suffer too much . . .' *Dio mio.*

Paula sat very still for a few moments. 'I cannot imagine what it must have been like to find his body – and in a holy place,' she mumbled in a shaky tone. 'Who would want to kill a Florentine priest, especially someone as kind as Father Gianni? It makes no sense.'

'Unless he had an enemy – a person who hated him enough to . . . kill him.' Raphael switched to Italian, speaking slowly for Paula's rather basic comprehension of the language.

Folding my hands in a quiet, prayer-like posture, I found my thoughts anything but serene. The images of Father

Gianni's death kept flitting through my mind, along with an impossibly bizarre train of thought. 'It may be that his murder – and it can be explained by no other word – is linked to the note about Allegra.'

They both remained silent.

Then Paula spoke up. 'But, Aunt Claire, how could those two events be connected? No one else aside from you and Father Gianni knew about the note; you did not even tell *me* until just now.'

'Perhaps he mentioned it to someone else – a person who did not want him to uncover any secrets and decided to kill him quickly to prevent further probing . . . I am only speculating, but how can I not draw a connection between the events, not to mention—'

A sudden loud knock on the apartment door reverberated through our rooms.

Startled, I whispered, 'Who could that be?'

'Signora Clairmont! It is I – Matteo Ricci, your landlord,' we heard the visitor shout. '*Come stai?*'

'*Sto molto bene,*' I exclaimed. Then turned to Raphael and continued in a low tone, 'We cannot afford to slight him. Help me into the parlor, so I can receive Matteo there, and I will speak to him alone while you question the driver. *D'accordo?*' As I held on to his arm, I managed to hoist myself upright. Surprisingly, my weak ankle seemed fairly stable.

Raphael and Paula stood on either side of me and paralleled my slow steps toward the parlor. Once I reached my usual wingback chair, I slipped into it, resting my head against the back cushion. My niece waited until I signaled her to let in our visitor, and Raphael disappeared into the kitchen.

I folded my hands on my lap and awaited Matteo's entrance. Listening to Paula exchange pleasantries with him, she gave no sign that we had just been discussing Father Gianni's horrific murder. My dear, brave Paula.

In a few moments, Matteo hurried into the parlor, his middle-aged, somewhat lined face drawn tight with worry. 'Signora Clairmont, I just heard that you fainted at the basilica. Have you recovered?'

'*Si.*' I extended my hand to him; he bent over it and placed a whisper-light kiss against my fingers. A lovely, oh-so-Italian gesture that I adored even after all these years living in Florence. It also felt normal. 'Thank you for your concern, Signor Ricci.'

He took a seat across from me as Raphael returned with a glass of limoncello, an Italian drink much favored by our landlord. Once he set it on the small, carved table next to my chair, he mumbled a greeting to Matteo and then exited with Paula.

'Pardon their quick departure, but Paula has . . . pressing issues with her daughter,' I said, smiling.

He inclined his head. 'Of course.'

Of medium height, with thick hair graying at the temples, Matteo had been our landlord for three years, and I found him pleasant enough, though not exactly warm in his manners. But he was the one who had hired Raphael for us, so I had to acknowledge his good judgment when it came to finding a protective, reliable helper. He also lived nearby at the east end of the Boboli Gardens and was quickly attentive to any needed repairs to our rooms. A typical Florentine in that he was civil, bordering on charming, yet there seemed to be something in his smile that did not quite touch his eyes . . . It had the cast of a man who was often hiding his true thoughts.

'I had also heard that you were the one who found Father Gianni . . .' He broke off and smoothed down the crisp pleat in his black trousers. 'It must have been quite an upsetting day for you.'

'Yes, it was quite a shock. As you know, Father Gianni had been a friend of mine for many years – such a good man in so many ways.'

'*Si – uomo buono.* A very good man.' Matteo murmured a short blessing in Italian. 'He heard my first confession, and I relied on him for his wisdom throughout the years.' Of course, as a member of an old Florentine family, he would have known Father Gianni for most of his life, although I had never heard him reference the priest with other than a passing comment. 'May he rest in peace with God.' Matteo crossed himself, ending with his hands in a brief, prayer-like position.

I mirrored his action solemnly, and we shared a few moments of silence.

'Father Gianni was my *parocco* since my arrival in Firenze years ago and, even more importantly, he was one of my first friends. I shall miss him dearly.' I heard the sadness in my own words. 'There is – or rather, was – no one whom I would trust more to hold a confidence or give reassurance.'

'So you were at the basilica this morning for confession?'

'Yes. I often go . . . the consequences of having lived such a long life.' I offered the ghost of a smile – I could summon nothing more. 'There is always a need to confess over some newly remembered episode from the past.'

He laughed. 'I heartily anticipate more of those as I grow older.'

'One can only hope.' Leaning my head back, I feigned a tired sigh. 'I may need to lie down and rest now, but thank you for stopping by. Your kindness is most appreciated.'

'By all means, I will take my leave.' He drained the last of his limoncello and slowly rose to his feet. 'I am very glad that you appear to have no lingering effects from your fainting spell – and, please, do not hesitate to ask for my assistance with anything that you might need. You know you can always count on me.'

'*Grazie mille*, Signor Ricci.'

He clasped my hand briefly and then saw himself out. Once I heard the door close behind him, I snapped my head up again and peered out of the window, pondering the *real* reason for his visit. He had been nothing but congenial in our past acquaintance, but his unexpected appearance and deliberate questions had roused caution inside me.

I closed my eyes again, not pretending fatigue this time. I *was* exhausted, worn out from the traumatic events today. Certainly, I had seen death in many forms over my lifetime, but never murder. *Never that.* I needed some rest to restore myself . . .

The next thing I knew, someone was gently shaking my arm. 'Wake up, Aunt Claire.'

'I must have dozed after Matteo's visit,' I murmured to myself, my eyelids slowly easing open.

'Did he stay long?' she inquired as she and Raphael sat down.

'No – only a few minutes,' I said. 'In truth, I do not completely understand the reason for his visit, aside from questions about Father Gianni's death. I related nothing but the barest facts.'

Paula's brows knitted in response. 'Do you think he believed you?'

'I believe so, but I am not sure what he wanted to hear. His queries seemed innocent enough, but then again . . .' My voice trailed off in doubtful caution. I gave myself a mental shake. 'What did you find out from the carriage driver?'

'We located the driver next door, waiting to take Signora Carlino to the cobbler,' Raphael chimed in. 'He told us that he did not recognize the man who carried you out of the basilica – it was not one of the priests but might have been a British tourist . . . one he had seen who was buying Italian artwork from a dealer who is well known in Firenze.'

Paula and I exchanged glances, whispering, 'Mr Rossetti?'

'*None so.*' Raphael lifted his hands in a gesture of uncertainty. 'We cannot know for sure.'

'Aunt Claire, what exactly did you and Father Gianni discuss?'

Taking in a deep breath, I realized that I would have to share the remaining pieces of my story. 'When I met him yesterday, I gave him a letter that Byron had sent me years ago, turning down my request to see Allegra after he had placed her in the convent. It seemed so cold and heartless at the time, even though our relationship had long cooled. It was a brief note, but Father Gianni seemed quite interested in some marking of a burner that I had not noticed—'

'*Como?*' Raphael cut in swiftly.

I explained the drawing of the charcoal burner on Byron's letter.

His face lit with sudden realization. 'The Carbonari – that is their symbol.'

'Who?' Paula turned to him with a puzzled expression.

Raphael leaned forward, resting his elbows on his thighs. 'The Carbonari were a brotherhood of revolutionaries who fought to unify Italia decades ago; they were part of the uprisings against King Ferdinand in the 1820s. Some say their group had been around long before that, shrouded in secrecy, but the records are sketchy since they disbanded after Pope Pius issued a condemnation against them. All we know is they played a part in bringing our country together when they were most needed.'

'But why the charcoal burner?' she persisted.

'It symbolizes their brotherhood, including workers who were from the trade of charcoal-selling, known as "men of wood" – they often met outdoors in remote locations,' he continued. 'If Byron had that image on his letter, it means that he was probably a member of one of the secret societies – they were very active around Ravenna and may have recruited him.'

Paula turned her glance to me again. 'It is true? Did you know he was one of these Carbonari?'

I shook my head. 'We were not on good terms at that time. I was living in Pisa with Mary and Shelley, while Byron stayed in Ravenna with his new mistress, Teresa Guiccioli. But rumors of *her* family's involvement in revolutionary activities were well known. Certainly, we were all interested in Italian revolutionary politics, but maybe Byron took it a step further and was actively participating in the brotherhood. The only thing I *do* know is he did not want Allegra living with him while he resided in Ravenna.'

'Where is the letter?' Paula queried.

Still feeling somewhat dazed by Raphael's revelations, I searched my thoughts for a few moments. 'I . . . I believe that Father Gianni had it when I found his body. Before I fainted, I retrieved the letter and slipped it in my purse.'

'I'll get it,' Raphael immediately offered and disappeared into my bedroom. Barely a minute or so elapsed before he returned with my black velvet drawstring purse adorned with a gold tassel. He handed it to me.

Loosening the strings, I hunted around for the letter but came up with nothing. I flipped the purse upside down and dumped the contents on my lap. A few *lire*, an embroidered handkerchief and a small comb tumbled out – but no letter. 'I am sure that I placed it in my purse. Then again, I was so

overcome by emotion that I may have dropped it on the floor.'
Shoving the items back in my purse, I jerked the strings tightly.
'We must find the letter and work out if there is a connection
between Father Gianni's death and this unsettling information
about Allegra—'

'It all started with Mr Rossetti's visit,' Paula cut in. 'Maybe
he followed you to the basilica.'

'We cannot know that for certain, but his appearance seems
to have set something in motion.' I paused, fingering the gold
tassel. 'He wanted an answer about selling my correspondence,
so I think we should give him one – just maybe not the one
he was seeking.'

Paula eyed me speculatively. 'What did you have in mind,
Aunt?'

Slowly, carefully, I began to lay out a plan . . .

After a long discussion, we decided to ask Mr Rossetti to meet
us at the Uffizi Gallery at ten o'clock the next morning. It was
one of the most public places in Florence, and with its magnificent artwork it would, no doubt, appeal to him as a meeting
place. Safe and aesthetically pleasing. Then, once we connected
with him, I would signal Raphael. He would appear – seemingly
unplanned – with the driver who could identify whether Mr
Rossetti was indeed the man who carried me out of the basilica.

At that point, if we needed to, we could call in the *polizia*.

'Perhaps we should question him ourselves?' Raphael proposed.

More discussion. We agreed to let that part of the plan
unfold – at least until after we knew for certain the facts about
Mr Rossetti's role in the drama earlier today. Going over the
details several more times, Paula eventually brought over my
quill and paper for me to write the note inviting him to meet
us at the Uffizi.

Holding the quill for a few moments, I gathered my thoughts
before I began writing.

Dear Mr Rossetti,
    I must apologize for ending our talk somewhat abruptly
during the last time that we spoke. However, I have had
time to consider your proposal to purchase some of my

letters from Shelley and Byron. If you are still interested, perhaps we could discuss this matter further? I shall be at the Uffizi Gallery around ten o'clock tomorrow morning on the second floor near Titian's *Venus of Urbino* and would be most happy to meet with you.

Gratefully yours,

Claire Clairmont

Signing my name with a flourish, I blotted the ink and then handed the missive to Paula for review. She scanned the document with lightning speed and gave it back to me with a sly smile.

'*Eccellente.*'

I folded the note and sealed it with a wax impression of my initials. 'Raphael, can you deliver it this afternoon?'

'I will do it now – and wait for his response.'

He took the note and strode out of the parlor, stopping only to give Paula a chaste kiss on the cheek. It was the first time he had shown his affection for her openly in my presence, and my niece blushed as he exited.

'Do not be embarrassed, Paula,' I urged. 'Love is not something that should be hidden or cause one to feel ashamed. I never did and would not ask you to, either.'

'I did not think that I could care for anyone again after Georgiana's father left us – without even a proposal of marriage or a backward glance. My feelings had turned to stone, but then Raphael came into our lives, and I realized that I had never truly experienced love.' She paused as a glow lit her delicate face. 'I suppose even the most hardened heart can melt under the light of true love. Raphael told me he feels the same, so what harm is there in that?'

'None at all – he has proven himself to be loyal in the last few days.' I now believed in him, although I had had some initial doubts. He would always be there for Paula – a protector. Sadly, that was something I never had in my journey through life. No father and no husband to care for me in the dark times. I was always alone, but that would not be Paula's fate.

My glance fell on the book of poetry that I had perused only a day or two before. Yet it felt almost a lifetime ago when my thoughts had absently drifted back to the words that Byron had written about me during the Geneva summer. My poem. My precious poem. More valuable than anything that had been given to me because it immortalized our love and what he had felt for me during that brief time when we shared our lives together.

So the spirit bows before thee / To listen and adore thee . . .

I had been adored; what more was there in life?

'Not to bring up unpleasantness again, but what do you *really* think about Father Gianni's murder?' Paula posed. 'It could be a coincidence, of course, that he was killed on the morning that you met with him. After all, Italy is a country full of passionate people who often pursue the vendetta – and it can turn deadly. Perhaps one of his parishioners became enraged about a perceived slight and decided to take matters into his own hands.'

'A murderous wrath against Father Gianni?' I said in disbelief. 'No – he was incapable of eliciting that kind of emotion. Trust me, he possessed the soul of a truly religious man, and the whole of Florentine society idolized him, including me. It could not have been a crime of anger.'

'Then it was a planned killing,' she finished for me. 'Carefully thought out and executed without mercy.'

Oh, my poor, dear friend.

'An assassin.' Blinking back the tears, I struggled to find the words to continue. 'Father Gianni must have possessed some piece of information that put his life at risk, whether it was connected with Allegra or not. He heard many confessions during the course of his life as a parish priest; perhaps a guilty secret had been revealed to him that he should not have known. Yet I feel his death *must* be connected with Allegra and Mr Rossetti's visit . . .'

'As do I.' Paula squeezed my hand. 'Shall we have tea? That old blue teapot still has some life in it, I think, and Georgiana should be back shortly.'

I nodded as a knock at the door caused us to turn our heads simultaneously.

'Ah, that should be her with Maria's mother.' Paula headed for the door, and before I could smooth down the folds of my dress, Georgiana skipped into the room carrying her doll and humming under her breath.

I held out my arms and Georgiana climbed on to my lap. My sweet great-niece. She so reminded me of my own daughter.

As I cuddled Georgiana in my arms, she began to sing *'Maria Lavava'* – 'Mary Busy with the Washing' – a nursery rhyme that I had taught her by singing it first in Italian, then in English. It was one that I had sung to Mary and Shelley's children many times during my early years in Italy when I took care of William and then little Percy, who was born in Pisa. I wanted them to know the regional *filastrocche* – children's songs so they had a sense of the beauty of the Italian language.

My memories took a sad turn as I recalled that, after William died and Allegra was lost to me, I had only Percy to teach the traditional Italian songs. A fair-skinned boy with sandy-colored hair, he possessed the sweetest temperament when he was young – so like Shelley himself.

> *Stai zitto mio figlio,*
> *Che adesso ti piglio*
> Hush my son, my little one
> In a moment I'll have done . . .

It was Percy's favorite song . . . and he sang it over and over.

My thoughts drifted back to that time when we were living at Le Spezia, a coastal town on the Adriatic Sea, in a mystical, dreamy seaside villa that was the last shared home for Mary, Shelley and me. Unfortunately, those final bittersweet days lasted only a short time before Shelley was drowned at sea, and our little group scattered to the winds as if fate had deliberately chosen to rip apart the thread that tied us together.

So many years had passed since then and so many people had passed out of my life that it sometimes folded the present into the past, and I felt the shadows creeping around me again – ready to engulf my senses if I did not keep myself rooted in the lives around me. The here and now. Still, the music of Percy's song never left me.

Le neve sui monti
Cadeva dal cielo,
Maria col suo velo
Copriva Gesù.
As snow from the heavens
Fell over the mountains
With her mantle of blue
Mary covered Jesu.

My voice caught on those last lyrics, even though Georgiana seemed blissfully unware of my reaction. The 'snow from the heavens' had a melancholy tinge in spite of being a child's song, and it made me remember that even a joyous pastime could turn tragic with a blink in time.

Like Shelley's death.

He had been sailing with Edward Williams on his dearly beloved sailboat, the *Don Juan*, and was swamped in a storm. We knew when they did not return that we would never see them again. But we could do nothing but wait until their bodies washed ashore – which they did ten days later. Both Shelley and Edward had to be cremated instantly on the beach to the south where they lay, a funeral pyre that neither Mary nor I could watch. But the black smoke rose up so high we could see it from our villa – and smell the acrid, sour odor of charred flesh.

Trelawny had organized the whole thing and, supposedly, reached into the fire to grasp Shelley's heart for Mary to keep forever.

I never saw the heart, but Trelawny had repeated the story to me many times.

That is when the tragedy takes on a mythic shade of eternal loss.

A poet's life snuffed out before his time – yet also the loss of a husband, father and friend.

Georgiana dropped her doll and screeched, jolting me back to the present. Easing her off my lap, I retrieved the doll and gave it back to her. She hugged the little moppet closely and danced off to her room after giving me a hug.

The sweet joy of youth – I would protect it with my life for as long as the innocence could last.

Paula strolled back with a tray and set it on the tea table. 'I hope Georgiana did not wear you out too much after your horrendous morning. You must not overdo it, Aunt. You have experienced a major trauma.'

'I promise to pace myself, but being with Georgiana infuses me with energy. I never feel tired after being in her presence. Never.' My eye flicked over the blue teapot as Paula poured the steaming, dark liquid into china cups. 'Indeed, she gives me the courage to take on our meeting with Mr Rossetti.'

'Do you think he will agree to meet us?' she inquired. 'Perhaps he will want a more private meeting place, especially if his motives are not honest, though I can scarcely believe he would have anything to do with Father Gianni's death.'

'Nor I.' Picking up the cup, I held it up for a few moments in contemplation. 'Then again, we know little about him. Outwardly, he seemed most interested in my letters from Byron and Shelley, and anxious to see my rightful place in their history restored. In truth, our conversation was pleasant enough until I became upset over having been omitted from Shelley's latest biography.' Slowly, I drank my tea. 'He never caused me to believe he had a sinister motive, but men can hide their true natures behind the social niceties.'

'We must be very careful how we proceed, for all of our sakes.' She briefly looked over her shoulder in the direction of her daughter's room, and I noted the tremor in her hand as she poured another cup of tea. 'We must protect Georgiana at all costs.'

'Do not worry, my dear. We will triumph – I promise.'

After resting in the late afternoon, I had an early dinner and then went to bed just after sunset. Surprisingly, my slumber was deep and restful, and I awakened feeling quite invigorated and ready to take on the day's adventure. I had half expected to be haunted by nightmares of Father Gianni's sad final moments, but that did not happen. Instead, I had only sweet dreams of Allegra running toward me, laughing and holding out her arms.

And I was not the only member of the household energized by a good night's sleep.

By the time I completed my toilette, Raphael had already called for my carriage driver of the previous day and Paula had taken Georgiana to her friend Maria's house once more. Then the three of us set off for the Uffizi Gallery an hour before we were due to meet Mr Rossetti. Although we spoke little, I sensed that both of them felt the same combination of fear and excitement that had stirred inside of me. My world had changed from the boring dreariness of living in genteel poverty to the anxious hope of grasping for a lost dream. I accepted all of it gladly, since it meant I would finally know the truth about Allegra's fate.

And now I also wanted to know who had killed Father Gianni.

Glancing up, I said a brief prayer for my old friend as the sun beamed down with a hot, bright intensity. I did not know how the day would end – I could only hope for some type of reckoning that would bring the truth to light.

I felt a soft hand on my arm.

'Aunt, we have arrived,' Paula said gently. 'Are you certain that you want to go inside? Raphael and I can do this alone—'

'Nonsense. I am perfectly capable of doing what needs to be done.' My chin went up in stubborn refusal to give in to any weakness. 'I have traveled half the world on my own; I can handle one Englishman in a public setting.'

Paula laughed and gave me a quick pat. 'I forgot whose presence I am in today – you are not the type of woman to ever give in, and I love you for that.'

I kissed her cheek. 'Let us go inside then.'

Raphael helped us both out of the carriage and we stood there for a moment, admiring the beauty of the building before us. I had strolled through the gallery countless times during my life in Florence, and it always took my breath away when I beheld the long, narrow courtyard lined by rows of columns that stretched toward the Doric screen, and then the Arno River behind it. Symmetry and beauty. A sixteenth-century monument to both the practicality of politics (it originally housed Florentine magistrates) and the wealth of the Medici family. Many far-reaching laws had been decided within the Uffizi walls, ones that affected the lives of people who lived here.

Now it was known for its magnificent gallery, which contained the extraordinary genius of the many artists who had walked these streets. The stunning altarpieces of Giotto, painted with all the religious reverence of his soul. The elegant Madonnas of Filippo Lippi. And the mythological allegories of Botticelli. I knew them all so well.

But I chose to meet Mr Rossetti near Titian's *Venus of Urbino* – the sensual, vivid odalisque that had charmed me in my youth. It was one of Shelley's favorite paintings because he always said it celebrated the beauty of the female body in a pagan manner. Venus lying on the soft chaise, her gaze direct and sensual, ready for surrender yet demanding respect for her sexual power. A woman for the ages.

Pondering my choice, I could not resist an inward smile as we made our way up the stairs to the second floor of the gallery. *Venus, indeed.*

We strolled down the corridor, lined with artwork and magnificent Roman statues, passing the occasional tourist who appeared to be transfixed by a particular painting. No one spoke very loudly in the presence of such visual brilliance, but I still caught the occasional comment in English about a 'stunning brushstroke' or 'shadow and light' – in homage to the artists who created such beauty.

Reaching room twenty-eight, we peered inside and found the space empty of tourists – and of Mr Rossetti. Perfect. Paula and I could position ourselves in front of the Titian painting and send Raphael back down to fetch the driver. We could engage Mr Rossetti in conversation, and then let the driver identify him (or not) as the man who had carried me out of the church yesterday.

That was our plan.

It could not fail.

Once Paula and I moved to the far end of the room, near the Venus painting, we told Raphael to bring up the driver in half an hour. His young face grew tight with worry, but Paula urged him on, whispering, 'You must do this – for me.'

He nodded, then left, with a last glance at us before he disappeared.

'Are you ready?' she asked me.

'Yes.' Clutching my purse to keep my hands from trembling, I would not allow my niece to see my anxiety. 'It is nearly ten o'clock. If Mr Rossetti is on time, we will have to engage him in conversation until Raphael comes back with the driver.'

'That should not be a problem, considering the beautiful art that surrounds us.' She swept a hand across the room, ending with the *Venus*. 'Your choice of this painting was deliberate, I assume?'

I glanced up again at the sensual depiction of femininity and smiled. 'Of course. We will have the advantage in our deliberations with Mr Rossetti since he cannot help but be somewhat distracted by Titian's . . . artistic skill in depicting the female form.'

We both laughed, but it had a high-pitched, nervous sound even to my own ears.

The nearby church bells rang out, and I realized the hour had come. I would know the real reason for Mr Rossetti's visit. Glancing at the doorway, I could feel my heart beating against my chest and, for a moment, I had a mad desire to run from the room. I longed to know why he had come to Florence, but I also could not bear to hear that it was not connected to Allegra at all. Only a mother's unlikely fantasy.

Just then, Mr Rossetti strolled into the room, and I reached for Paula's hand. She gave my fingers a squeeze of encouragement, and I took in a deep breath.

He approached us with a few quick, easy strides and a friendly greeting. 'I am delighted that you consented to see me again, Miss Clairmont.' He gave a brief bow. 'I must apologize again for upsetting you during our first meeting; it was certainly not my intention. Your ankle is much better, then?'

'Yes, thank you for asking.' With a critical eye, I watched him carefully as Paula chatted with him about the beauties of the gallery. Certainly, his first impression appeared confirmed: a pleasant, typical British tourist. Impeccable black coat and trousers with a carefully tied cravat. Neatly combed hair and trimmed beard. Relaxed demeanor.

Nothing about him bespoke anything but the most open intentions.

I listened intently as their discussion switched to the paintings, especially the lovely Titian behind us. More pleasantries and, surprisingly, he did not seem unduly diverted by the *Venus*. All of a sudden, it felt as if the room was shrinking inward, the walls closing in on the three of us . . . the paintings murmuring secrets from the past.

'Miss Clairmont?' he was saying.

'Pardon me, I was lost in thought – the infirmities of old age.' I pulled a small fan out of my purse and opened it, fanning my face. 'I tire more easily, even in the presence of such masterpieces.'

'It is *my* fault – I should not have kept you standing this long.' He ushered me to a small bench, and I eased on to the seat with a sigh of relief. Unfortunately, our plans for the encounter with Mr Rossetti this morning had not taken my aging bones into account. Or the time it would take for Raphael to return with the carriage driver.

'I am happy to continue our chat from this lovely bench.' I patted the space next to me, and he seated himself on the bench. Paula remained standing nearby, keeping a watchful eye on the door for Raphael. She appeared calm, but I noted her flushed cheeks and the slight tremor in her hands, mirrored by my own. I managed to continue in a quiet tone, 'The Titian *Venus* was one of Shelley's favorite paintings; he was most inspired by the beauties of art – especially those that depicted ancient myths.'

'Ah, yes. His reputation as a scholar of antiquities has certainly become widely known from the latest biographies . . .' He halted awkwardly, no doubt realizing that he had moved on to the subject that had thrown me into such distress the last time we met. 'I . . . uh . . . did not mean to broach the subject again—'

'There is no need to be so tentative, Mr Rossetti. In spite of my age, I am not such a frail flower that I cannot hear the truth,' I assured him. 'In the last few days, I have come to accept that I am gradually being relegated to a bit player in the dramas of my youth. Biographers worship the famous and snub the obscure. That is the way of the world, is it not? But that in no way alters my financial situation. I need to sell my letters, and you want to buy them. So we are bonded by mutual need.'

He gave a slight inclination of his head. 'Miss Clairmont, you amaze me with your openness and honesty. I cannot imagine there is another woman alive who has such a direct manner.'

'Well, I suppose there are few women who have achieved the seventh decade of life at all. Once women no longer resemble the deliciously decadent *Venus*, we must take on other qualities that make us . . . fascinating. Besides, there is nothing unfeminine about plain money talk.'

'You have my attention,' he said, glancing up at the *Venus*. As he did so, I locked eyes with Paula, who gave a slight grimace as she pointed at the door.

'Since we seem to understand each other, Mr Rossetti, shall we move on to business?' I prompted, still fanning myself.

'Indeed.' He turned slightly, so that he faced me, still seated on the bench. 'As I stated a few days ago, I am interested in any letters that Shelley or Byron wrote to you as part of the research for the Shelley biography that I am currently writing. I can pay handsomely for the letters – and I promise to avoid any . . . delicate subjects, shall I say?'

'I have nothing to hide; then again, I do not wish to expose Paula and her daughter to any censure over my youthful indiscretions.' Choosing my words carefully, I did not want to give Mr Rossetti any reason to think I was not being absolutely honest in my dealings with him. 'Very few people outside of our intimate circle know about . . . my daughter, Allegra.'

His expression remained unchanged – polite and bland. 'I had heard that you had a child with Byron, but I see no reason to include that fact in my biography, should you prefer to omit it.'

'I am most grateful because, as you may or may not know, Allegra died at the Convent of Bagnacavallo when she was quite young – and, though I rarely spoke of her, I do not wish for her memory to be sullied in any way whatsoever.'

'I agree wholeheartedly.'

Would he have this reaction if he had placed the note about Allegra under my teacup? Was he so impressive an actor? Or was he truly here simply to purchase the letters?

'You realize that losing a daughter was the great tragedy of my life?' I prompted, sensing Paula move to stand behind me. A sense of comfort flooded through me at my niece's lovely gesture; I never needed to worry about her not accepting any aspect of my life. She had much of my brother Charles's strength of character.

'I can only imagine, Miss Clairmont,' he said. 'I do not personally have any children, nor do my brother or sisters. Sadly, we are all childless – much to our parents' dismay. But I can imagine how you must have mourned the loss of your daughter.'

Noting that Paula had begun tapping her toe on the wood floor with a tense and jittery staccato, I kept babbling away about the heartache of losing a child. Mr Rossetti simply nodded and said nothing. As the minutes passed, I became more and more convinced that he knew nothing about the Allegra note, which meant he was unlikely to have any connection to Father Gianni's death.

But I was determined to keep chattering until Raphael finally returned with the driver.

Mr Rossetti raised his hand. 'Miss Clairmont, if I may be so rude as to interrupt, I have something to show you before we discuss our transaction.'

I raised my brows expectantly.

Just then a group of Italian children ran into the room, followed by their young teacher who kept shouting, '*Aspetta! Aspetta!*'

They ignored her and swarmed around the room like flitting birds – chattering in Italian and shrieking with delight, and they jumped up and down on another bench. The teacher clapped a hand against her forehead, and then brushed back a lock of thick, dark hair from her face.

I tried to focus on Mr Rossetti's words, but he was drowned out by the loud, boisterous children.

'Could you speak up, please?' I urged him, but I caught only bits of his conversation: words like 'family' and 'legacy' and 'painting.' My jaw clenched in frustration but, if anything, the children's screeching grew louder.

Standing up, I shouted, '*Stai zitto!*'

They instantly quieted, staring at me in tearful shock.

At that moment, Raphael appeared in the doorway with the carriage driver, who immediately pointed at Mr Rossetti and exclaimed in Italian, 'It is him. *He* is the one who carried the old woman out of the cathedral.'

I gasped.

Old woman?

Everyone in the room (including the children) turned to Mr Rossetti, whose face had begun to turn various shades of red.

'Is that true?' I queried. 'Did you follow me into the Basilica di San Lorenzo yesterday?'

He stared at the floor. 'Yes.'

'Why?' The word caught in my throat as Raphael rushed to our side, dragging the driver along with him. 'I would like an explanation, please.'

'We *all* would,' Paula added.

Sighing, Mr Rossetti looked up again. 'I have been trying to tell you that I came here not only to buy your letters but also to convey something else that I discovered only recently in the papers of my deceased uncle, John Polidori.'

'John Polidori was your . . . uncle?' My legs gave out, and I sank back on to the bench, dropping my fan to the floor.

Mr Rossetti retrieved it. 'I thought Trelawny told you in his letter.'

'He did not.' Dazed, I took the fan from him.

'I cannot think why he held that piece of information from you since I made no attempt to hide it from him. I would never have been so interested in writing Shelley's biography were it not for my uncle's association with him – and Byron.' He paused, blinking rapidly. 'I am somewhat dismayed at this turn of events.'

'As am I, sir.'

That past had truly come back to haunt me – and in a way that I'd never expected.

Polidori.

Captain Parker's Log
April 10, 1815
Bima, on the island of Sumbawa (forty miles east of Mount Tambora)

We docked the Fortuna *in Sape – a port on the eastern side of Sumbawa – late this afternoon, a hot and sticky day that caused our breathing to turn heavy and labored as my men and I handled the rigging. After reassuring my nervous crew, I went ashore alone to obtain provisions before we set sail for the west side of the island tomorrow morning. Unlike our usual shore excursions, this one had my men preferring to remain at dock, tending to the ship. In truth, they had been uneasy for the last two days, knowing that we were setting out for Tambora. I had heard their murmuring on deck, which would abruptly cease the moment I approached. Then once I had passed them by, the low voices would begin mumbling the same phrase again and again:*
   Mountain of Fire.
   Mountain of Fire.
   It sounded almost like a chant – or a prayer for God's protection.
   I cannot say that I blamed my crew for their caution. Even though the volcano explosion had taken place days ago, the air still had a dank, oppressive feel. Even worse, the acrid smell that permeated the air grew stronger and stronger as we drew closer to Tambora. None of us spoke of the odor, but we all knew what it meant. The Mountain of Fire had spewed its flames into the atmosphere, perhaps even burned all life around it. There was little I could do to assuage my crew's fears – just keep them focused on the task of trimming the sails and keeping the rudder on a steady course.
   Once we had arrived at Sape and the Fortuna *was safely docked, they calmed slightly, and I went ashore to purchase supplies from a British quartermaster named Mr Kincaid who lived in nearby Bima. Making my way to his office, which was perched on a hill above the small*

*town, I sweated and cursed for most of the climb. Rural
and sparsely populated, the mountainous land around
Bima held an eerily quiet feeling, as if it were waiting
for the next move of nature's chess game, though the
Tambora eruptions had passed. We were all pawns, I
supposed, in the face of the awesome power of the
Mountain of Fire, but I was determined to stock my ship
and set sail again – survivors' lives could be at stake.*

*Once I met Mr Kincaid, I found him to be a most
congenial quartermaster and host. Young and energetic,
he quickly arranged for my ship's provisions and
confirmed that Mount Tambora had erupted five days ago
but, apparently, caused little destruction or loss of life
on the east end of the island. No one had received word
from the western shore, but he felt most of the villagers
had time to escape the volcano's fury. A minor hope
stirred.*

*After I sent word to my first mate that we would
leave at dawn, Kincaid invited me to join him for dinner.
I found the prospect of a meal on* terra firma *held a
huge appeal for me after the weeks aboard ship,
partaking of only the most basic foods, and he did not
disappoint me.*

*In his two-storied home near the supply office, he and
his charming wife set a table of local fish, fresh vegetables
and tropical fruits that included mangos and papaya –
sweet and ripe. I ate my fill and more – enjoying the
pretty features of my hostess and witty conversation of
my host. It felt so civilized after the months on the* Fortuna.
*Over post-dinner port, we all moved on to the wide
veranda and gazed out over the town below in the twilight.
Small houses with thatched roofs dotted along the coastline, tiny dwellings adorned with thick patches of palm
trees. Beyond that point, the sea barely stirred a gentle
swell along the surf.*

All quiet.

*It began to drizzle and we moved under the awning,
still chattering away most happily, until I noted the raindrops seemed more like tiny pebbles. Not ash, but stone.*

Kneeling down, I picked up a small piece of rock and frowned when I realized it was made of pumice.

Then I heard a deafening roar like a blast of mortar fire, booming with a monstrous thunder from the west. The house shuddered violently as if the ground were shifting underneath, and the large multi-paned windows rattled.

'Get inside – now!' Kincaid shouted as his wife cried out in fear and covered her ears.

Another blast cracked out, even louder, and I could hear screaming from the residents in Bima below as the pumice stones rained down – harder and thicker. A hail of rocks and fury. The sky darkened abruptly, turning from gray to black in seconds. More blasts followed in rapid succession . . . booming with a deafening roar.

For a moment, I felt paralyzed by my fearful thoughts. Pulse racing, throat tight . . . I was fixed to the spot.

Then Kincaid shouted my name and urged me inside again.

Shaking off the panic, I followed Kincaid and his wife inside the house, feeling the floor tremble under my steps. The three of us positioned ourselves next to the interior stairway as we held on tightly to the rail. Mrs Kincaid wept silently as she leaned into her husband, who circled his arms around her in a protective embrace.

'Tambora is erupting again,' Kincaid said in grim voice as pictures that had hung on the wall shattered on to the floor.

My ship – I needed to get to the Fortuna *and see to my crew, as well as the cargo. I could not lose everything after we had come this far.*

My men depended on me.

SIX

Castle Chillon, Montreux, on Lake Geneva, Switzerland, June 1816

I could not resist the lure of Castle Chillon.

As Byron and Shelley planned their sailing trip around Lake Geneva – a literary pilgrimage to Rousseau's novel *Julie* – Mary and I initially thought we would be invited to accompany them. But it rapidly became clear that the men wanted to take this expedition alone. We loved sailing just as much as they did, with the feel of the wind against our backs as we mastered the challenge of a starboard tack. So why not ask us as well?

Silly of me, but I was jealous.

Not over the loss of Byron's presence; I had gradually come to accept that our relationship might not have the permanence that I had once sought so passionately. I coveted the adventure. Why should we not enjoy the beauties of the lake simply because we were women? And our exclusion was not because of my 'delicate condition,' since neither Mary nor – surprisingly – Polidori had revealed my pregnancy to the other members of our circle. If truth be known, it seemed as if the poets wanted to experience this trip without having to bother with 'female vanities,' as Byron termed it.

Maddening.

Undeniably brilliant, Byron could also be annoyingly conventional in some of his views regarding women.

Of course, Mary accepted this fact with her usual grace and equanimity, but I was not so agreeable. I wanted to see the eastern part of the lake – especially the magnificence of Chillon, a medieval fortress that stood on a flat rock, its towers and battlements extending out over the water, almost as if it were floating on the surface. An island of rock and power. It had stood guard over the lake for centuries, and I wanted to see it for myself and imagine the memories of wars and lost generations that had seeped into the stones and settled into dust during the long years as time passed. And I wanted to share it with Byron before *he* slipped away from me, which was beginning to feel inevitable, in spite of our unborn child.

I realized that if I made the land passage to Chillon, they would have no choice but to let me accompany them in the sailboat for the return trip. It would be worth it to risk the overland journey around the lake – and the prospect of Byron's anger – just to have those few magic days of sailing along the lake with the men whom I most admired and loved. It might only last as long as a whisper in the wind, but I would make that moment last a lifetime.

I told Mary that I was going to stay with a friend in Geneva for a few days and engaged passage on a public conveyance to take me around the eastern side of the lake, along the road to Montreux. Byron and Shelley had planned to be there by the end of the week, so I had time to make my overland journey, which I calculated would take two days. A simple plan for a woman with the courage to follow her heart.

Mary accepted my proposed trip into Geneva without question because William was, once again, ailing and she was most concerned about her son's frail health. Polidori had left us for a brief visit with Madame de Stael in Coppet (a most welcome absence), so I did not have to confront his razor-sharp curiosity about my movements.

All of fate seemed to align positively for my journey, and I could not have been happier when I set out.

Unfortunately, it proved to be an arduous trip. I had not counted on the rough, brutal nature of the lakeside road. It jarred every bone in my body and caused my back to ache as I absorbed the impact of the rocking carriage. There were but three of us in the vehicle – an older Swiss couple and me – and we all held on to the seats with white-knuckled grips for hours upon hours. A gentle, misting rain followed us like a shadow, cold and dreary. But I refused to turn back. When we finally drew near Lausanne, we discovered that a massive shower the night before had washed out a large section of the road, and we had to walk half a mile as the carriage went around on an alternate route that proved to be too rough for passengers.

It had turned dark by the time we reached Lausanne – a tiny hamlet at the northernmost part of the lake. But I was so enchanted with the rolling hills and miles of vineyards that I felt somewhat restored by dinnertime at a modest hostelry, even so far as to enjoy a pleasant meal with the couple who shared my carriage. Peter and Marianne – middle-aged Swiss residents who peppered their conversation by interrupting each other good-naturedly – were heading back to their home in Zurich after a jaunt to see their daughter and grandchildren in Geneva, and we all toasted our triumph at reaching the halfway point to Chillon without a broken bone.

After they retired, slowly moving up the stairs, hand in hand, I felt a tiny sting of sadness. Would I ever have a loving husband who looked at me the way Peter gazed at his wife? Or was I doomed to forever be struggling alone?

I did not dare answer that question as I looked down at the slight swell in my abdomen.

The next day, we received a lucky break in the weather and were able to cover the distance to Montreux by early evening. The driver left me at a modest lodging near the shore of Lake Geneva, and I bid my travel companions farewell as they continued on to Zurich.

As I trudged toward the hotel entrance, carrying my own small bag, I took in the smattering of small houses along the lake and the slightly dilapidated appearance of the public house with its crooked shutters and chipped paint: the Hotel Montreux. It was the best that I could afford, even though the town boasted only one other place to stay, from what my fellow travelers had told me. Shelley often referred to villages around the lake as 'wretched spots,' which seemed a bit too strong, although the poverty of this area was in contrast to the relative wealth of Geneva.

After checking in, I retreated immediately to my room, partaking of a light supper of bread and butter, then dressing for bed. The room had a slightly shabby look that matched the hotel's exterior, but a large window overlooked the lake, and I could vaguely make out the shoreline in the growing dark. For a few brief moments, I thought I saw the sun slide out from behind the layer of clouds – a bright, jagged slash of light that faded as quickly as it appeared.

Sighing, I leaned my head against the window frame as I felt the presence of the child inside of me, the stirring of new life. Yet it was not a sense of joy that came with it. Instead, doubts swirled in my mind at the sudden realization of my foolish behavior in coming to Montreux. Why could I not be temperate in my actions? Byron would probably be angry when he saw me; Shelley would be full of consternation. They would then argue, with Shelley taking my side. But I would get my desire to sail back to Geneva with them, eventually. And that is what I wanted, was it not?

If I had not seized the opportunities that passed my way, I would still be living in my stepfather's house, waiting for my life to begin, hoping and praying that I would partake of love's joys.

Should the child turn out to be a female, is that the lesson that I would teach my daughter? Jump into the volcano and never look back? Shaking my head with a laugh, I turned away from the window and lay on the narrow, lumpy mattress. Who knows? Perhaps my own child would have a wisdom that I never possessed and not need any such lessons about life. I could only conjecture at this point. All I knew was that I had no intention of ever reining back my impulsiveness, no matter what happened. I would always choose risk over restraint. Truly Byronic, in my own way.

Closing my eyes with my hand still covering my stomach, I drifted off to a hard, dreamless sleep and awoke to the sunshine streaming across the room. My mouth curved into a sleepy smile.

Light and love.

A good omen.

Quickly, I completed my toilette and donned a freshly washed dress of pretty white cotton with tiny yellow daisies embroidered on the material. Thank goodness the fashion of the day still boasted a high-cut empire bodice which hid my expanding waistline, though even I had to admit that my condition would be undeniable in a few weeks' time. Byron needed to know the truth, and soon, before it became self-evident or Polidori told him. But I would not think of that today. The morning was too beautiful, the day too sweet for me to cast any gloom over my own happiness.

Packing up my belongings, I paid my bill and set out to stroll the short distance to Chillon along the lake, noting how the brilliant blue of the water reflected a matching sapphire tint in the sky on this sunny morning, so refreshing after the unrelenting weeks of rain. I had almost forgotten how vividly colorful the lake's surface could appear on a clear day.

I nodded at the occasional passer-by, but it was the many natural charms of this rural part of the lake that absorbed most of my interest: wildflowers blooming in profusion along the path – pink and yellow and purple, all with varying balmy scents – stirred by the light breeze rustling through the tall pine trees with a soft, hushed echo.

Every step brought a new sensation of delight.

Dreamily, my mind drifted like a feather in the wind until I arrived at Chillon – a graceful, powerful testament to the Middle Ages. Walls of white stone. Towers of varying heights that soared above the ramparts. Tiny, slit-like windows on every level. It thrilled and beckoned from where it had stood guard since antiquity between the Great Saint Bernard Pass and Lake Geneva.

I was enthralled not only by its majestic beauty but by my own audacity.

This place was perfect. *I will tell Byron about our child – here and today.* The castle's walls had seen much history and witnessed many secrets, so my revelation would be but a link in the long chain of human drama that had occurred in this place. But it was my moment. I had become a prisoner of the heart, rather than the body – not chained to my famous lover but tied to him, nonetheless.

Today, the truth would be out.

I did not know what would come thereafter, but I could not hold this secret for another day.

As I moved through the entrance into the open-air courtyard, I gazed around for a *gendarme*, but the place seemed empty. I called out to announce my presence but received no answer. Although the castle had long been abandoned as an actual fortress or a prison, surely it still drew visitors because of its history and association with Rousseau?

'*Allo? Allo?*' I exclaimed.

A door slammed behind me, and I started. Then I glanced over my shoulder and spied an elderly man slowly descending the stairs from the watchtower.

'*Bonjour, Mademoiselle,*' he said.

'*Monsieur.*' I shielded my face from the sun overhead, but still had to squint to see him in the bright midday light.

'You are English?' he switched to my native language with an ease borne of long practice.

I nodded.

Reaching the bottom of the stairs, he motioned for me to follow him. 'I assume you want to see the dungeon. Everyone who comes here wants to see the pillar where Bonivard was chained.'

'Indeed, I do.'

'*Bien.*' He moved toward a small stone archway, motioning for me to follow. 'François Bonivard was the prior of Saint-Victor in Geneva. He would not renounce his Protestant beliefs when the Catholic Counts of Savoy ruled this area, so he was imprisoned within the dungeon walls below for years, chained to a pillar, until the Bernese liberated him. His captors would have freed him instantly if he had only declared his allegiance to the Pope, but he refused. And so he remained in his chains.'

A captive of his faith.

I shuddered, following him with reluctant steps, realizing that when Rousseau referenced Bonivard's name in his book *Julie*, I had simply read it as a historical note. I never truly understood the extent of the prisoner's sufferings.

After we entered the archway, I groaned inwardly when I spied the steep descent of narrow stairs. I could not take a chance on slipping and possibly hurting my child, but as I beheld my aging tour guide easily maneuver the steps, I felt somewhat heartened. I wanted to see this dungeon more than ever now.

Gripping the uneven wall, I turned sideways and eased down the stairs. 'Are you the lone caretaker?'

He nodded. 'I spend most of my days showing tourists the

dungeon and making minor repairs so the castle does not fall into complete decay. You see, there is no one who will commit the funds to keep this old building from crumbling into the lake.' He ambled past the rows of Gothic pillars that arched upwards to support the soaring, vaulted ceiling. 'It was once a fortress, then a prison; now it is largely abandoned, used only for storage of wine and grain. A sad fate for this grand old castle . . .'

As we reached the lower floor, the air took on a distinct chill; I pulled my shawl tighter around me and wrapped my arms around my waist.

Carefully negotiating the interior cobblestones, then strolling past the barrels and grain sacks, I came to a halt next to my guide in front of a massive pillar at the end of the long row of seven columns. A rusty iron hook, embedded in the stone, stuck out from one side – and my eyes widened as I touched it.

'Was this where he was chained?' I whispered.

'*Peut-être.*' He pointed at the long, narrow window carved out in the upper wall with a grate affixed to it. 'Bonivard said he could look out of the window when he was a prisoner and see the waters below. Apparently, the sound of the waves lapping constantly against the castle walls almost drove him mad.'

All of a sudden, I noticed the steady beat of the waves: soft and rhythmic, the rolling surf had a soothing quality to me because I could climb out of the dungeon at will. If I had been imprisoned and forced to listen to the lapping waves, I might have been driven to madness myself.

'How did he finally escape?' I inquired.

'The Bernese forces captured the castle and set him free – a happy ending for him, at least, though he had a brother who did not survive. He had to watch him die.'

Tears stung at my eyes as I swung my glance back to the iron hook, imagining the horror of Bonivard's captivity. The iron chains that bound him. The days and nights of despair. The moment when his brother took his last breath. My breathing grew ragged as these images flashed through my mind . . . and I slid awkwardly on to a large piece of rock.

'*Mademoiselle*, are you all right?' He extended a hand in my direction, but I waved him off.

'I am fine – just need a few minutes to compose myself. This is a most distressing place, and I was expecting something more . . .'

'Romantic?' A wry smile touched his aging face.

'*Mais oui.*'

He shrugged in a typically Gallic manner. 'We often want our stories to be tied up neatly with the good rewarded and the evil punished, but I fear that in life that happens all too rarely. Even though Bonivard was released, nothing could ever erase the years and years of his suffering, or the loss of his brother.'

'You are a philosopher, *monsieur.*'

'No. I am merely an old man. I have seen much of life and learned to accept what comes, no matter what.'

Glancing around the dungeon, I could feel the weight of centuries of living and breathing men who never saw the light of dawn again. 'I wish I could claim your equanimity to the vagaries of life, but I fear I, too, am a prisoner – of my own passions. But perhaps that is simply my nature, and I must be true to it.'

'Experience has a way of taming our youthful waywardness.' He extended his hand again and I took it, allowed him to help me stand. His eyes moved over my stomach, then met mine in gentle understanding as he continued, 'But perhaps you already know that.'

Did he discern that I was expecting a child?

'Hello? Is anyone here?' A familiar male voice rang out from the courtyard above. Shelley. He and Byron must have arrived in their sailboat.

Finally.

My tears and melancholy mood instantly vanished, replaced by a beaming smile – a fact not lost on my tour guide, no doubt.

'*Un moment,*' the old man shouted back, though he kept his glance on me. Then he squeezed my fingers in reassurance. 'Come up when you feel like it; there is much to see here at the castle, and I shall have a light refreshment for you before you leave.'

'*Merci.*' I kissed him on both cheeks.

Turning on his heel, he climbed the stairs and exited the

dungeon. I strained my ears to hear what he was saying to Byron and Shelley, but I could make out only Bonivard's name and not much else. Of course, they would want to see the prison cell first. But I was not ready to reveal myself yet. Looking around for a place to hide, I tucked myself behind several of the large wine barrels stacked in the corner of the prison room.

I heard their voices touched with a sense of awe as they descended into this dank, gloomy chamber; the caretaker had not accompanied them.

'How could anyone keep a sense of humanity in this depressing prison?' Shelley was saying in a hushed tone. I could hear his light footsteps in a rapid staccato on the stairs.

'I believe I already know the answer to that question,' Byron responded, his gait much slower due to his clubfoot. 'I have been shackled to the darkness of my own mind for as long as I can remember – and that is no place for the faint of heart, I can assure you.'

'I am assured of nothing, except you are a better man than you portray to the rest of the world – or to yourself.'

Byron laughed. 'If only everyone had your kindness of spirit, my dear Shelley, we would not have oppression *or* prisons, such as poor Bonivard suffered at Chillon. But I do not expect that I shall see humanity take on such merciful qualities in my lifetime.'

'You may be pleasantly surprised yet.'

'I shall await that day with much anticipation, my friend.' Byron's words held a note of indulgence. 'Which pillar was he chained to?'

'The one, I believe, at the far end of the dungeon, or so the old man just told me,' Shelley responded as their voices trailed across the dungeon, becoming fainter as they moved further away from my hiding place. 'Seven pillars, seven years . . .'

I could not make out the rest of Shelley's words.

From my kneeling position, I craned my head around the wine barrels in an effort to eavesdrop on the rest of their conversation, but I could catch only random phrases that made no sense to me. Easing back again, I crouched down, my weight on my heels. As the minutes passed, my legs began to grow painful and stiff, causing the muscles to contract with tiny spasms. I had to reveal myself – soon. I did not completely understand my reluctance, but I felt caution . . . for the first time in my life.

Perhaps I had been rash to come here after all.

'I want to see the upper levels of the castle,' Shelley was saying as their voices moved in my direction again. 'That is where Rousseau wrote about Julie's son falling into the lake—'

'Did she not plunge in after him in the novel?' Byron queried.

'Indeed, yes. She saves her child, but then catches a chill and dies. A life for a life, I suppose – the ultimate dilemma. My lord, would you risk all for your own child?'

Awaiting Byron's response, my hand moved to my stomach as if it were a protective shield. I did not need to ask myself that question; I already knew the answer.

'We must all eventually die, my dear Shelley, but we must go and stand in the place where Julie dived into the lake and pay honor to her sacrifice, as well as to Rousseau's novel that has so inspired us.' Byron mumbled something else under his breath that I could not hear, but I heard Shelley respond that he would meet him in the south tower. Then I heard footsteps on the stairs.

Byron had remained in the dungeon – alone.

After listening to the lapping waves in silence, I heard an odd scraping sound. Peering around the grain sacks again, I saw Byron chipping away at one of the pillars with a pocket-knife. His head tilted down, frowning in concentration, he jabbed the blade at the pillar repeatedly. Stone chips flicked to the floor as he chiseled away.

'Why are you here, Claire?' he asked, without turning away from his task.

Slowly, I rose to my feet.

Byron kept chipping at the pillar. 'Did you really think that I could not smell your fragrance from the moment I entered the dungeon? Roses do not grow in this dank, dark place – only moss and dandelions.'

Of course. He had often remarked on the cologne that I wore and said it reminded him of the English roses that grew around his ancestral home and filled the air with sweetness. I moved toward him, and still he did not face me.

Coming to a halt behind him, I surveyed his work. He was carving his name on the pillar: Byron. Only that – and nothing more. 'Do you think this pillar will give you the immortality of Bonivard?' I queried.

He gave a short laugh. 'He endured more suffering than any one man should ever face in one lifetime; I do not think I could ever equal that. No . . . Bonivard's name will linger through the ages, and I do not expect that I will be known much past my own lifetime.' His tone turned sharp and bitter as if he were chipping away at his own immortality.

Leaning my forehead against his back, I remained motionless until Byron finished his task.

Then I straightened and surveyed the jagged lettering now etched forever on the pillar – the letters slanted downwards and diminishing in size, but his name was clearly visible as an homage to Bonivard. 'Perhaps there is another type of immortality.'

He finally turned to me, his eyes bleak as he slipped the knife in his pants pocket and allowed his glance to slip to my abdomen.

He knew.

Biting my lip, I glanced down to hide the tears. 'So you guessed?'

'Claire, I am not so stupid as not to sense when a woman is expecting a child. I suppose it is mine?'

Jerking my head up, I blurted out, 'How can you even ask that? I have been only with you.'

'My apologies, my dear, but our relationship in London was brief, ephemeral even – almost as if we were passing each other on the way to a new life – and I never asked for you to be exclusively mine.'

'But I have been faithful to you.' Searching his features, I could not find the truth of his heart. 'Were you not to me?'

He averted his glance. 'I must remind you again that I was . . . and *am* married, though Annabella and I have been separated many months. As for other women . . . I have no desire to establish another permanent connection at present.' He twisted a lock of my hair around his index finger, then brushed it behind my ear with a gentle stroke of hand. 'I wish I could give you a promise of love and a vision of the future together, but that would not be honest. Those feelings seem dead to me, and whether they can be resurrected or not remains to be seen. All I can say is that I cannot give you what you seek now, only assure you that you are my *one* attachment—'

A cry of relief broke from my lips before I could stop myself. 'That is all I ask for now. That no other woman will supplant me in your affections while we remain in Geneva, or convince you not to accept our unborn child.'

He stiffened slightly.

'Albe?' I pressed.

Byron hesitated, then took my hands and folded them in front of me, covering them with his own. 'You know my reputation is in tatters; it will never recover. I am beyond redemption in the public's eyes. But you are still young and have a chance of a respectable life, in spite of our connection here. You are William Godwin's stepdaughter and could manage to re-establish yourself in his household should you decide to return home without Mary and Shelley or a child . . .'

'What are you saying?'

'Give birth in secret and leave the child with some local family. You can then return to England and beg to be back on good terms with your mother. She could arrange for a match with a man of good standing—'

'No!' Pulling my hands away, I stepped back. 'I do not feel the least bit of remorse about anything that I have done. My life is my own. What kind of existence would I have in a marriage to a man I do not love? Modest and decorous. Those are not words that have any appeal for me,' I scoffed. 'Mary and I know we are already ruined, and we chose this path.'

A shadow of concern flitted across his pale, handsome face. 'There is no going back if you keep the child.'

'I know.'

He turned silent.

'You still do not understand me,' I said in a tense voice. 'I do not possess the genius of Mary or the wealth of Shelley's family, but I am my own woman. I may not have fully under-stood the import of my actions in the past, but I do now, and I choose . . . freedom. I would rather have the disapproval of the whole world than live a life that is not my own.' My breath came in ragged gasps as if I had run a great distance. 'Or is it only men who can have that kind of *carte blanche*?'

More silence.

Then Byron finally spoke. 'So be it.'

He reached into his pocket and retrieved the knife. 'You might as well carve your name beneath mine because you have made your choice. At the very least, I suppose Bonivard would be proud.' He offered me the blade with a ghost of a smile in his eyes – sad and proud and lost. All of a sudden, I saw my future reflected in his gaze.

I would never be accepted by society.

I would never marry.

I would never have security.

Freedom would cost me dearly.

Taking the knife from him, I kissed him lightly on the lips. 'I'll join you and Shelley directly.'

'We will await you in the courtyard.' He pivoted on his good foot and limped toward the stairs.

After he made his way out of the dungeon, I swung my attention back to the pillar and angled the knife under Byron's name. Grinding the blade's edge against stone, I carved my first name boldly, each letter carefully etched into the pillar: *Claire*.

Surveying my work with a grunt of satisfaction, I realized that something had happened to me today. What started out as yet another impulsive action – traveling miles and miles over rough terrain to confront my lover in a wildly romantic castle – had somehow been transmuted into a journey toward maturity and motherhood. Hereafter, all of my decisions would be made with my child uppermost in my mind, but as an independent woman.

I slipped the knife in my bag, knowing it would be a cherished memory, long after these days had passed. A forever moment.

With one last glance through the window at the shimmering lake that stretched below, I began to climb the steep steps that led out of the dungeon, careful not to slip on the uneven surface. Reaching the top, I attempted to clasp the wall to steady myself and touched . . . someone who stood in the recess. 'Byron?'

I swiveled my head in his direction, but before I could say any more, I felt myself tipping backwards, desperately clutching at the figure who remained in shadows. Screaming for help, I tumbled down the stairs, feeling the hard impact of each rocky step before I slipped into the dungeon's abyss.

I felt a tap against my cheek. Then another – and another.

Stop it, I wanted to protest. But I could not manage to utter the words; something was preventing me from speaking. Or opening my eyes. It felt like a heavy, suffocating blanket covering my face, muffling my senses, pinning me down. Panic spurted through me, racing through my veins with dread. Was I being suffocated?

My eyelids fluttered open, but as I beheld Mary's familiar worried expression, I relaxed again. She was touching my cheeks lightly with the back of her hand as she eased down the blankets that had been covering me.

'Where am I?' I managed a whisper, realizing that I was lying in a vaguely familiar large bed.

'At the Villa Diodati. Shelley and Byron brought you here two days ago.' She sat next to me on the bed. 'You had a high fever from your fall. Do you remember anything?'

I closed my eyes briefly and registered images of being jostled in a carriage, vaguely aware of the mountains and pine trees flitting past. Everything seemed hazy, as if I had dreamed it. 'Why was I brought here?'

'Byron insisted.'

'Was I with him?'

'You tumbled down the stairs at the Castle Chillon where you had secretly traveled to meet Byron and Shelley – a fact that you omitted to relate to me.' I heard the irony in her voice and felt a twinge of guilt.

'I apologize, Mary.' Rolling my head on the pillow away from her, I glanced at the huge tapestry of a medieval scene woven in gold and black on the wall. Byron's bedroom. I knew it well. 'It was impulsive and stupid of me to lie to you.'

'Do not distress yourself further, Claire. You have suffered enough.' She touched my arm, and I winced. Checking the source of my pain, I noted that my skin now had blotches of various shades of purple.

'You had some bruises and a deep gash where you must have hit a sharp rock on your fall,' she explained. 'They found you in the dungeon, barely conscious, raving that someone had pushed you down the stairs.'

I sat up abruptly, alarm flooding through me. Then my head pounded as if a thunderclap had struck the inside of my brain and I collapsed back on to the pillow. 'What about . . . the child?' Clutching the sleeve of her gown, I prayed that my baby was unharmed.

'Hush, now,' she urged. 'Byron called in a doctor from Geneva when you first arrived at Diodati, since Polidori is still at Madame de Stael's. The baby is fine.'

'Thank God. I could never forgive myself if I had killed the child with my foolishness. I will never again take a risk like that now that I am responsible for another life – I have to live for my offspring now,' I vowed, half to myself. 'I never truly understood your feelings over William's delicate health until this moment. Forgive me.'

She kissed my forehead. 'There is nothing to forgive.'

The world had righted itself again, if only for a short interlude.

'It was necessary for the doctor to know about your condition, which means Shelley and Byron also know,' she continued in a hesitant voice. 'I could see no other way to ensure that both you and the child were healthy.'

'Byron had already guessed.' The memories of what occurred at Chillon came rushing back: the eerie darkness of the dungeon, with its odor of stagnant water and sound of lapping waves. And the moments with Byron as he carved his name into the pillar . . . followed by my own chiseling of stone into immortality.

'The stairs must have been slippery from the dampness,' Mary said. 'It is not surprising that you slipped—'

'No.' I gasped. 'The stairs were steep, but that is not why I fell.'

An image of a figure stepping out from the shadows flitted through my brain. Then a sense of falling backwards. Then nothing.

'What are you suggesting?' Mary started, her eyes wide.

'I . . . I think someone might have pushed me down the stairs at Chillon—'

'Surely that cannot be,' she protested in disbelief. 'You are letting your imagination run wild again, Claire.'

'Indeed, I am *not*.' Grasping her arm, I struggled to make sense of the snippets of flashbacks. 'Byron and I were in the dungeon alone after Shelley had made his way to one of the high towers. After we talked, Byron followed him. I left soon after, climbing the steps that led into the main courtyard. But when I reached the landing, I caught sight of someone out of the corner of my eye. A figure hidden in some dark recess who reached toward me. Then I fell.'

Mary drew back, her face twisted in shock. 'But why would anyone want to do harm to you? Are you certain this phantom meant to shove you backwards? I can scarcely believe that a person could be so evil as to do something like that. But if it is true, then someone wanted to k–k—' She broke off.

'Kill me?' I managed to utter the words in a low tone. 'Why else would someone hide in the shadows and shove me?'

'Oh, Claire, an accusation like this against a local could have huge consequences for us since we live in Geneva under the protection of a suspicious Swiss government. Byron has publicly supported revolutionary causes, and there are spies everywhere who would be delighted to have a reason to expel us from Geneva. We must tread cautiously.'

'But I have no enemies here—'

'Perhaps you do if we are tainted by association. Your relationship with Byron is an open secret in Geneva . . . and remember when someone broke into your room at the Hotel d'Angleterre and smashed your locket?' Rubbing her forehead, Mary let out a long, audible breath. 'I do not know what to think at this point.'

'Nor I.' A disturbing thought drifted into my consciousness. 'What if my attacker was someone I know?'

'A member of our magic circle? Who?'

Steeling my nerves, I said the name aloud: 'Polidori.'

Mary shook her head. 'I know you and he have often argued, but that would hardly be cause for him to take such a rash and horrible action. Do you really believe he would stoop to murder you?'

I paused, realizing the accusation sounded absurd even to my own ears. Still . . . 'Who else could it be? I hardly know anyone else in the area, aside from our little group, since we keep to ourselves.'

'True, yet you may have inadvertently angered a servant or a tradesman,' she posed. 'An inner fury can be aroused by the most mundane of slights.'

Glancing nervously around the room, I searched my thoughts for some memory of a harsh exchange with a passing acquaintance, but I could find none. 'It *has* to be Polidori – I can think of no other person who has aroused my suspicions.'

'For God's sake, do not repeat those fancies,' she hissed. 'It will seem like hysteria to the men.'

Of course, she was right.

At that moment, Shelley appeared at the door like a beam of sunlight, practically glowing with the warmth of kindness. 'You are finally awake, sweet Claire. We were all most worried about you.'

Managing a smile, I motioned for him to join us. 'I am sorry for causing such a stir – truly, I did not mean to create havoc by showing up at Chillon and then . . . tumbling down the stairs. I must have slipped in agitation as I came out of the dungeon – such a gloomy spot. But I am fine now. Quite well, really.'

I could hear Mary exhale in relief.

'Chillon is a dreadful place, like a tomb that houses the lost souls of those who were imprisoned and hanged there. I could almost feel them around me as they took their last breaths when the noose tightened around their necks. The snap of bone and muscle.' Shelley's voice rose an octave as he pantomimed the process of being executed by a rope.

'Shelley, please stop,' Mary pleaded with him.

'Sorry, my dear.' Remaining on his feet, he took a place behind her and dropped a light kiss on her neck. 'I was simply agreeing with Claire that her fall was not her fault. It is a wonder that any of us emerged uninjured. She is to be only admired for being so brave.'

Mary's mouth tightened, but only I could see it. 'Some might say *rash* for making a journey there without any of us knowing—'

'Oh, no, it was irresistibly daring to want to see the castle that so entranced Rousseau,' he admonished her gently. 'There was a time when you would have done the same and thrown caution to the wind . . .'

'That was before we had a son,' she murmured under her breath, but I caught the words and understood only too well now. A mother's love was consuming.

'It was a foolish thing to do, and I would not risk it again,' I said in a firm voice.

'No matter the reason or outcome,' Shelley said, 'the important thing is that you are in good spirits, Claire – and none the worse for falling on the stairs. Although I will admit that we had grave misgivings when we found you on the floor of the dungeon.'

'Mary said that you and Byron conveyed me back here—'

'Yes.' Byron's voice wafted into the room as he appeared, leaning against the doorjamb with a casual posture. But his eyes looked strained and tired. 'We thought, at first, that you must have fainted in the damp air of the dungeon, but then we saw the scratches on your arms and guessed that you must have fallen down the stairs. It was a frightening realization. Then you developed a fever within a few hours, and we hired a carriage to bring you back to Diodati as quickly as possible. We did not know if you would survive the journey—'

'And the whole time, Byron never left your side,' Shelley added with wink in my direction.

Byron made a dismissive gesture. 'I could hardly leave you in the care of the caretaker at Chillon or a public carriage driver.'

'I am most obliged to you.' Turning my head, I extended my hand to him . . . and then saw Polidori next to Byron. Instantly, I drew back.

'We are all happy that you have recovered, Miss Claire,' Polidori joined in with a seeming note of sincerity that did not match his hard stare.

'Indeed,' Shelley enthused. 'And to celebrate, we must all convene in the drawing room tonight and have Mary entertain us with her ghost story—'

'No,' she protested. 'That is the last thing Claire will wish to hear in her weakened state.'

'Not at all – it would be a welcome distraction,' I assured her with a nod.

Shelley clapped. 'It is agreed, then: we shall meet this evening and Mary will read from her book – *Frankenstein*.'

I tried to summon a smile, but just then the rain began to pound against the windowpanes and the wind howled with a jarring, plaintive sound.

Was it the promise of things to come tonight?

Hours later, after I had rested in the afternoon, Byron returned and, without speaking, carried me down to the drawing room, bearing my weight with his muscular upper body. As we entered the drawing room, I noticed a roaring fire already blazing away, with Mary and Shelley huddled over some sheets of paper. Byron settled me on the sofa, then stepped back.

'You are comfortable, then?' He scanned me with a speculative gleam as if he were seeing me for the first time. Had my fall caused feelings of remorse in him? Was he thinking about our relationship differently now that he knew I was with child?

'I am.' Arranging the folds of my cotton dress, I took a quick glance around the room for Polidori. Thankfully, he was not in attendance.

Shelley brought me a small glass of sherry. 'You must keep the sparkle in your eyes, Claire. And no more secret trips out of our sight – it would not be safe for someone in your condition.'

I stiffened.

It had been spoken aloud and confirmed: the entire room knew that I was pregnant.

Shelley must have seen my reaction because he immediately glanced at Mary, who aimed a pointed stare at him.

'I . . . I apologize if I spoke out of turn,' Shelley stammered. 'It was not my intention to make you uncomfortable.'

An awkward silence fell upon us, and poor Shelley looked stricken by his own loose tongue, yet I did not blame him.

'Mary, are you still sharing your novel with us tonight?' Byron queried, helping himself to a glass of deep red wine. 'Shelley has told me of your powerfully evocative descriptions of nature – told by a monster who is brought back to life through the unholy scientific arts. Personally, when I am dead, I would prefer to stay dead. I do not want to experience more of the same wretched heartaches.' He threw himself into a wingback chair, crossing his boots at the ankle and staring down at his wine glass. 'One life is quite enough.'

'I cannot agree less, my lord,' Shelley interposed. 'I would be glad to enjoy ten lifetimes if it meant I could turn the world to goodness and light, especially with my poetry. It is the highest calling of human nature to be a poet . . . the unacknowledged legislators of humanity.'

Byron made a scoffing sound low in his throat. 'If only it were so. I fear no matter when I put my pen to paper, I feel only the darkest emotions erupt and I must get them out of my mind or I should go mad. Of course, it is possible that I am already mad like poor François Bonivard.' He paused. 'What do you think, Claire? Am I insane, as my wife and her lawyers seem to think?'

'Hardly. You have kindness in your deepest being. I know it and the world would know it, too, if only you would let them see the Albe who has been our host and benefactor this summer. You are far from a lost soul, believe me.' The words came spilling out before I could stop myself, hating to see him in this type of foul and black mood. He must have had a letter from Annabella's attorneys today – they always drove him into a fury.

'Perhaps we are all in Bedlam and simply not aware of it,' Mary reflected, her eyes growing clouded and troubled. 'I have long thought all creative endeavors have the possibility of leading us into such unknown lands of the imagination that we may never return to sanity and reality. It is the danger that all authors face.'

'Mary, you are the sanest person I know – a writer, a

companion and a mother,' Shelley assured her, and then turned to Byron. 'As for Albe, I cannot vouch for him.'

We all broke into a loud laughter that seemed to lighten the mood, as if Shelley had lit a candle in the darkness.

Byron inclined his head. 'I would not expect you to, Shelley.'

Just as he spoke, a loud clap of thunder announced that yet another violent storm was sweeping in off the mountains to the east. Flashes of lightning. Rumblings in the sky. It would soon follow. Then the rain would start up again in heavy, pounding waves against the windows.

Shelley glanced toward the large glass panes, his face kindling with excitement. 'You must read now, Mary, while the storm provides a perfect backdrop. Bring us into the world that you created – that of the living dead.'

'By all means, we must hear it,' Byron urged.

My own heartbeat turned into a rapid staccato in anticipation.

Slowly, she strolled toward the fireplace, parchment sheets in hand. Tilting them toward the fire's illumination, she cleared her voice and began to read. 'I had selected his features as beautiful. Beautiful! – Great God! His yellow skin scarcely covered the work of muscles and arteries beneath; his hair was of a lustrous black, and flowing; his teeth of pearly whiteness, but these luxuriances only formed a more horrid contrast with his watery eyes, that seemed almost of the same color as the dun-white sockets in which they were set, his shriveled complexion and straight black lips.' She paused, with a tremor in her hands, then glanced up. 'Shall I continue?'

'Yes, please!' Polidori entreated. I froze. He must have entered the room while we were all raptly focused on Mary's narrative, sliding into our company as if he were a snake slithering into paradise with every intent on bringing about the fall of humanity. He wished me harm – I knew it. But I had no proof that he had, in fact, pushed me down the stairs at Castle Chillon. None at all.

I had to remain quiet and calm.

My time to expose him would come.

Mary resumed reading in a thin, shaky voice. 'I saw his face bring on emotion . . . and he was alive!'

A huge gust of wind blew open the doors and every candle

in the room immediately went out, along with the fire. The room was plunged into darkness. Byron instructed everyone to remain still as he went for a servant. His boots made a scuffling sound on the hard, stone floor and then echoed out of the room.

Moments later, I felt a hand around my throat – a gentle clasp caressing my neck, but it was not Byron's touch.

I froze.

'You are fortunate to have survived the fall,' Polidori murmured into my ear. 'You must protect yourself at all costs so nothing like that occurs again.'

A match was struck and light filled the room again as Shelley lit a candle. He clapped enthusiastically over Mary's narrative, exclaiming it to be a work of considerable brilliance that would create a stir in the literary world. Blushing with pride, she made all the appropriate protestations, but her buoyant joy at Shelley's stream of compliments beamed out from her essence.

I, too, clapped – but kept a wary eye on Polidori.

His words held a warning, and I would heed it.

Miss Eliza's Weekly Fashion and Gossip Pamphlet
August 2, 1816, Geneva

The Ladies' Page
  Tragic news, dear readers: rumors have been swirling around Geneva that Lord Byron and his companions are soon to depart. It is all too true. Their time in our fair city is drawing to a close and, tragically, I have yet to catch a glimpse of the great poet himself.
  Oh, the unfair twist of fate!
  But never fear! After some scheming, yours truly decided upon a desperate move: to take an afternoon stroll through La Vieille Ville where Lord Byron often consults with his attorney (or so I have heard!).
  Ladies, I must remind you: the steep and crooked steps to reach the historic section of Geneva proved to be quite challenging, especially in the cold and rain, but I was determined to see the man who has set all of England ablaze with his scandals. And I made a promise to you,

dear readers, that I would do everything in my power to catch a glimpse of His Poetic Greatness.

And here is how it unfolded:

After loitering on La Vieille Ville for an hour, I took refuge in a tearoom near St Peter's Cathedral, with nothing to show for my efforts but rain-splattered clothing and sore feet. Ready to admit defeat, I began to make my way to the fashionable Rue de l'Hôtel-de-Ville when, en route, I tripped over the hem of my dress. (Yes, Miss Eliza has her clumsy moments.) As I pitched forward on the slippery cobblestones, I would have fallen except for a handsome man who reached out and seized my arm.

'Careful or you might twist an ankle,' the stranger said in a deep voice as I righted myself again.

Murmuring a quick and slightly embarrassed thank you, I realized with a touch of awe that my benefactor was none other than Lord Byron himself. Quelle surprise!

He disappeared quickly around the corner before I could pose any of the questions that you have been asking. Oh, the lack of quick thought! You can be sure, though, that I checked back and forth across the square with anxious eyes, hoping against hope that he might reappear.

But no such luck, ladies (sigh).

There you have it – the full and unvarnished truth of my encounter with Lord Byron.

It did not provide the results that I had hoped, but what in life does, dear readers?

But never fear that Geneva will become a bore . . . I have heard a famous English actress may grace our midst next week, and you can be sure I will have all the latest gossip!

SEVEN

Piazza della Signoria, Florence, Italy, 1873

We sat in a small outdoor café across from the Uffizi Gallery – Paula, Raphael, Mr Rossetti and I, quietly sipping a late-morning coffee as we all digested Mr Rossetti's revelation. He was John Polidori's nephew. I confess I was still rattled by the news.

When Polidori had died in 1821, I'd drawn a breath of relief, knowing I would never have to see him again.

I was safe – or so I thought.

As I sipped my coffee in silence, Mr Rossetti carefully placed a brown leather journal on the table. He fingered the embossed gold trim on the cover and smoothed out the curling corners with a reverent stroke of his fingers. Then he produced a silk handkerchief from his jacket pocket and dabbed it against his dome-like forehead. He seemed duly agitated by his own deception. Or perhaps it was something more?

I trusted him no more than I did his uncle.

He coughed lightly. 'Miss Clairmont, I should have revealed my connection to John Polidori when we first met a few days ago – my apologies. But Trelawny said he was going to inform you about the relationship. I cannot imagine why he did not say so in his letter unless he believed that you might not agree to see me, since you and my uncle had not parted on the best of terms, from what I heard.'

'When did you discuss this with Trelawny?' I queried, puzzled over my old friend's omission.

'In London – I had requested a meeting with him before I left for Florence.'

'I see.'

'I deeply apologize, Miss Clairmont, but let me explain my kinship to Polidori. This is his journal.' Flipping open the volume, he pointed at an ink-drawn family tree on the first page. 'You see, here is John Polidori and his sister, Frances; she is my mother. She married my father, Gabriele Rossetti – an exiled Dante scholar from Italy – and they had four children: my brother, the poet, Dante Gabriel, and my two sisters, Christina and Maria. So all of what I told you about my siblings is true. We never really knew our uncle, except through the stories that my mother would tell about him, because I was born eight years after he died. And the family connection at the time of his death was not exactly friendly – he was quite erratic at that point in his life from all accounts – and my mother grew even more detached from his memory when she learned that his cause of death was probably suicide.'

I cast down my glance briefly. 'I had heard the same thing, and it distressed me.' Indeed, in spite of Polidori's possibly malicious actions toward me, I had felt a pang of regret when I found out that he had ended his own life. A sad last moment for anyone.

'When I told my mother that I wanted to write a biography about Shelley and the circle of friends from my uncle's youth, she gave me his journal, which she had kept hidden since his death.' Mr Rossetti stretched out his hands across the table in appeal. 'I did not know how you would react to any of this information, so I asked Trelawny to contact you first. My declared intention for being here is honest: I came to purchase your Byron/Shelley correspondence, which I need for my research.'

'What exactly do you know about your uncle since he was not discussed much, by your own admission? He was not kind to my aunt.' Paula drew Polidori's journal across the table towards her and flipped through the yellowed pages. The jagged writing scrawled across the pages had faded over time into a faint echo of the original words.

'For that I am sorry, but I know very little except the barest details of his life as Lord Byron's physician and, later, as a man of literary aspirations.' A ghost of a smile touched his features. 'It's been said that I slightly resemble him.'

Scanning Mr Rossetti's middle-aged features, I tried to see past the veil of time: the Polidori that I knew was a young man. I saw little of his classically Italian comeliness in his nephew, except perhaps the eyes. Dark and smoldering. Polidori's stare could harden like bits of stone when he felt slighted, whereas Mr Rossetti's gaze had none of that type of arrogance.

'Nothing more?' Raphael added to Paula's question.

'Only what I have been able to find out myself from his friends and enemies who are still alive – and the journal.' Mr Rossetti's mouth curved into a slight smile. 'My mother is a very devout Catholic who did not approve of her brother's life – or death. It was, for her, an unpleasant subject that she rarely touched upon, so I have nothing from her. She still refuses to speak about him, though she might to her priest.'

'I understand.' And I did. As a converted Catholic, I knew only too well that my adopted religion allowed only for minor infractions, though I could hardly cast stones at anyone else's sins.

Raphael signaled for the waiter to bring us *fette biscottate*, though Mr Rossetti brushed off the biscuit-like hard bread when it arrived shortly. I broke off a large chuck and nibbled on it gratefully to ward off the lightheadedness that was overtaking me at every new revelation about our British visitor.

I needed time to grasp the impact of these details.

My gaze drifted across the Piazza della Signoria towards the beautifully symmetrical arches of the colonnade that stretched in front of the Uffizi. So beautiful and solid and enduring. How could anything be amiss when beholding the stunning Renaissance architecture of Florence? But, of course, the history that surrounded this piazza was anything but dull and routine – filled with years of conspiracies, as well as long-standing vendettas.

Tourists had begun to gather in small groups outside the gallery, eagerly chatting and gesturing at Michelangelo's sculpture of David that stood in the middle of the square. Graceful and elegant. A testament to art and liberty. Rumor had it that the original statue would be moved indoors shortly; for now, though, it stood proudly in all of its glory.

Unfortunately, I could not say the same for myself. Still reeling inside, I could barely sort through all of these recent revelations. 'For some reason, Trelawny withheld information from me and, while I believe your intent was honorable, given the family connection to Polidori, I am not sure that I can have any future dealings with you,' I began, choosing my words as if I were stepping over sharp stones on an unfamiliar path.

'Indeed, yes.' Paula's delicate features were drawn tight with caution.

'In my fervor to gain your confidence, I may have behaved thoughtlessly.' He cast down his glance, murmuring apologies in both English and Italian. The latter made little impression on Raphael, who now held Paula's hand very tightly in his own grasp, as if he were afraid to let her go.

'Apparently, you had even followed me to the Basilica di San Lorenzo when I met my priest—'

'No!' he exclaimed, his face turning up again with forceful denial. 'Yesterday morning, I had arranged to meet an acquaintance at the basilica to look at the frescoes, when people came rushing out, saying that an Englishwoman had fainted inside. I ran in and found you – the *polizia* had already arrived and were examining the priest's body. I swear on the life of my mother that is the truth. I carried you out and conveyed you back to your residence out of only the purest motives. Truly.'

Paula and I exchanged glances of doubt but, after his recent revelations, I was inclined to believe him about *this* part of his story. Giving a slight nod, I gestured for him to continue.

'I appreciate your forbearance, Miss Clairmont,' he said, folding his hands on the table. 'Granted, I should have remained with you and your driver, but the sight of the dead priest had shaken me greatly, and I returned to my rooms quite agitated. The sight of a stab wound will not be easily forgotten.'

Shuddering inside, I echoed his sentiment. *Nor by me.*

'You should have stayed, Mr Rossetti.' Paula wagged her finger at him with a jerking motion. 'My aunt was almost delirious at that point; we were fortunate that the driver stayed with her until Raphael could go down to the carriage and assist her upstairs. Poorly done, sir.'

'My behavior was unforgivable. I can only hope to make it up to all of you.' The sincerity in his voice rang true, though my own ability to discern anyone's true motives was in question after the events of this week. His presence at the basilica *could* have been a coincidence – the Medici church was, after all, one of the most visited sites in Florence. Then again . . . he wanted my letters more than anything.

Could I trust him?

Could I afford not to try – especially when he might have been the one to put the note about Allegra under my teacup? I dared not ask him about that yet.

'Our association with you, Mr Rossetti, is shaken, if not finished,' Paula blurted out as she shoved back her chair, but I placed a restraining hand on her arm.

She paused.

'My niece speaks impulsively, Mr Rossetti, because she cares for me so deeply,' I said, keeping my tone even. 'Perhaps you could *earn* our trust again – by being totally and completely honest about the scope of your research thus far.'

His face brightened considerably. 'It is more than I deserve, and thank you.'

Releasing my niece, she settled into her chair warily, and I did the same. 'I know you wish to purchase my letters – especially those written during the summer of 1816 – and you have Polidori's journal here.' I slid it back across the table toward him. 'What else have you acquired?'

'I have a few of Mary's and Shelley's letters that I already bought from Trelawny, along with interview notes from the younger Percy Shelley about his mother. As for research on my uncle, I have recorded some of his old friends' recollections about him – quite sad really. He was apparently overcome by depressive thoughts for many years and, I fear, made very little sense before he committed suicide. He talked much of his lost literary ambitions and how his novel, *The Vampyre*, was actually published under Byron's name, even though my uncle wrote the story—'

'Truthfully, Byron wrote the fragment after he proposed we all write a ghost story,' I interjected. 'He then gave it to Polidori to finish since he became too preoccupied with his poetry to compose a work of prose.'

'Ah, yes,' Mr Rossetti enthused. 'I know Byron's poems

well from that time – *The Prisoner of Chillon* and the third
canto of *Childe Harold*; they are magnificent.'

Inclining my head, I agreed. 'But Polidori *did* write the
novel, although Byron had the idea first – inspired by his
reading of Coleridge's *Christobel*. I even remember the
particular evening at the Villa Diodati when Byron recited a
few paragraphs from the tale.' Flashes of his melodious voice
floated thought my mind – a song from the past that I had
never forgotten – as he described a creature who sucked the
lifeblood from his victims. 'I assume the publisher thought to
trade on Byron's more famous name . . .'

A smile touched Mr Rossetti's face. 'Fame can cause people
to behave in unsavory ways – as you and I have already
discussed, Miss Clairmont.'

'How true. Fame can become an elusive dream, or a nagging
intrusion into one's life. But what I find most disturbing is
how it can cause a distortion of reality when it is manipulated
by those who want to change the facts.' I drained the last of
my coffee and slowly set the china cup on the saucer. 'If I
decide to proceed with a sale of my correspondence to you,
Mr Rossetti, I would like an assurance that the content will
not be altered in any manner to place me in an unfavorable
light.'

'*Che cosa?*' Raphael's face kindled in confusion. 'You
would still consider doing business with him?'

'I agree with Raphael.' Paula regarded the older man across
the table with a skeptical squint. 'With all due respect, sir,
you seem quite rash; I do not believe that you will use my
Aunt Claire's letters with fairness and impartiality. She has
been much maligned in the past and does not need any further
damage to her reputation.'

'You see how they protect me?' I smiled, quite warmed by
the love of my niece – and Raphael. 'I would be quite lost
without them, and I do, in fact, share their caution about any
"editing" of my letters. I do not want to be erased from history
as seems the case in the new biographies.'

'I vow to be truthful in all of my dealings with you, as you
are with me.' He placed a hand over his heart with a solemn
expression. 'If you would consider selling your Byron/Shelley

correspondence, I promise not to let my connection to John Polidori affect how I write my own biography of Shelley, including your role in his literary circle. I also intend to edit my uncle's journal – honestly and frankly with no bias against you.'

Weighing his words, I took a quick glance at Polidori's journal. Was it possible there was something in there about Allegra that even Mr Rossetti missed? 'I must consider this matter carefully but, as a gesture of goodwill, perhaps you could lend the journal to me – only for a day or two, I assure you.' Noting his hesitation, I continued, 'Trust goes both ways, does it not?'

Mr Rossetti picked up the journal and held it for a few moments in a tight grasp. He handed it to me. 'Yes, it does, Miss Clairmont. I am entrusting you with my legacy. And I will add that when I found you at the basilica, I also found a letter from Byron. I placed it in the back of my uncle's journal for safekeeping.'

'*Grazie.*' Sighing in relief, I slipped out Byron's letter – the one that I had given to Father Gianni. It was mine again.

Then my fingers closed around the journal and a tiny thrill shot through me: I held the book that was penned by the man who had haunted my thoughts for decades. Perhaps I would learn the story behind Polidori's dislike of me, and maybe even find a clue to Allegra's fate. It struck me as ironic that Polidori was there in the early days of my relationship with Byron, and now his presence had appeared again near the end of my life.

Strange, but somehow fitting.

'I will send word to you tomorrow when I have reached a final decision about the sale,' I said, clutching the journal against my chest. 'That will provide me ample time to read the journal.'

And perhaps learn the secrets that Polidori took to his grave.

'Is there anything else you need from me, Miss Clairmont?' Mr Rossetti asked.

I stared at him for a few long moments. 'No.'

Mr Rossetti gave a nod of assent, then took his leave.

We remained in the café for another hour as Paula and

Raphael tried to talk me out of any future dealings with him.
But I remained firm, adamant in my course of action. I would
have my way in this business, no matter what came of it.

It was time to learn the truth.

As I lounged in our sitting room at the Palazzo Cruciato that
afternoon, I barely suppressed a yawn as I adjusted my spectacles. Paging through Polidori's journal entries from 1816
had turned out to be a surprisingly boring narrative of his
self-inflated ego and petulance – typical of the man I knew
fifty years ago. Every line somehow defeated the beauty of
his subject by inserting his own sarcastic quips. A poor showing
as a writer, indeed.

His rambling account of Byron and his journey from England
to Switzerland in late spring had no sense of awe at the landscape. Just tedious details. Dull observations about a church
in Antwerp. Monotonous descriptions of a play he attended
in Brussels, complete with snide remarks about the acting and
run-down theater of peeling paint and dirty floors. Even a
place as poetic and evocative as the Waterloo Battlefield
sounded as if it were a potato farmer's plot.

Not surprisingly, his jealousy of Byron also came through
in almost every sentence, as when he referred to himself as
'a tassel to the purse of merit' (presumably, Byron was the
'purse,' though I did not want to pursue the meaning of
the 'tassel'). *Poor Polidori.* He wanted so desperately to be
famous.

He hated Byron, yet loved him – as did we all.

My mouth tightened as I reread Polidori's entry upon our
first meeting in Geneva and his rather unflattering portrait of
Mary, Shelley, and me: *P.S., the author of Queen Mab, came;
bashful, shy, consumptive; twenty-four; separated from his
wife; keeps the two daughters of Godwin, who practice his
theories; one LB's.*

Damn him.

Shelley did not 'keep' us, nor were he and I lovers, although
I knew it had been rumored during the time (and later). Shelley
was my dearest friend, my confidante, but *never* my *amour.*
I would have to discuss this passage with Mr Rossetti – if he

published the journal – so it was not taken as the 'truth' of our relationship during that summer. I could not allow the distorted ramblings of Polidori to be uncontested.

The rest of Polidori's entries were snippets of his disagreements with Byron over details of their life at Diodati. More yawning.

As I turned the pages in rapid succession, skimming over the mundane and the muddled details, I halted abruptly at the dates June 23 to 26 – or lack thereof. There were *no* entries during the three days when I had traveled to meet Byron and Shelley at the Château de Chillon and fallen down the stairs. Why had he recorded nothing on those dates? Then, on June 27, he made no mention that I lay ill at the Villa Diodati – only that he spent time with Mary and me in pleasant conversation. Needless to say, I did not quite remember that time as 'pleasant.'

Was the omission deliberate?

Mixed feelings surged through me. Why had Polidori concealed my accident? Or my pregnancy? He knew by that time, since he had told me he guessed my secret. I set the book down momentarily, letting my thoughts settle before I proceeded. All of these old memories had been buried for so long that they seemed more like echoes from an empty grave – no real form or reality aside from the fragments that I could piece together. Even without the chaotic events of the last week, I would have found them upsetting to recall.

Raising the journal once more, I flipped the pages forward with a reluctant hand, scanning the entries to see if there was any mention of my relationship with Byron – or our child.

'Aunt Claire, you must rest,' Paula said as she strolled into the room, Georgiana in hand. My great-niece came running over and slipped her arms around me, her small hand grasping my cotton dress tightly. I stroked her fair hair, the journal immediately forgotten as I beheld Georgiana's sweet, loving face.

Paula took the book from me and set it on the fireplace mantle. 'You have been reading and rereading that journal for hours – too much strain on your eyes, if you ask me. Besides, it is time for tea. I sent Raphael to the baker for biscotti, and I assume you wish to have oolong in the old blue teapot?'

I raised one brow. 'You need to ask?'

She laughed and sat across from me, bidding her daughter to sit on her lap. Georgiana immediately launched herself on to Paula's thighs and began to play with her mother's hair, spinning the long locks into spiral curls. 'Did you find anything surprising in the journal?' she asked, gently pulling her tresses out of harm's way.

'Nothing too unusual – except a few omitted days from that summer of 1816. I have my suspicions as to where Polidori had gone during that time, but he does not reference anything that would confirm my hunch.' I filled her in on the visit to Castle Chillon, including the mysterious tumble down the stairs and my feverish days afterwards. Her expression stilled, then turned grim with a deep frown.

'Do you actually believe he traveled to Chillon to . . . *harm* you?' she whispered over her daughter's head, keeping the volume just out of the range of Georgiana's hearing.

I shrugged. 'He may have followed me there and, when he found me emerging from the dungeon, saw his . . . opportunity. I do not know – maybe I simply did fall. That time was fraught with such emotion that I scarcely knew what I was doing. My world was starting to crumble because I knew Byron would leave me . . .' I glanced deliberately at Georgiana, seeing the image of Allegra in her. 'I had others to think about at the time, so my mind could have been clouded.' Closing my eyes, I rubbed my forehead as a wave of weariness overcame me. Bone-tired, emotionally spent fatigue sighed through my body.

'So the journal might just be the tedious recordings of a vain man, and Mr Rossetti has shown up in Florence exactly for the reason he stated. Could it be that simple?' Paula rested her chin on Georgiana's head with a sigh.

'But what about the note that stated Allegra lived? And Father Gianni's murder shortly after I asked him to locate the convent records about her fate?' I shuddered. 'That would be a huge coincidence indeed—'

'Signora Clairmont?' A booming male voice shouted outside

our apartment as a fist banged on the front door. 'It is I –
Matteo.'

I started, as did Paula, at the sudden shouting of our
landlord.

'Let him in – but give me the journal first, please.' I held
out my hand.

Paula eased her daughter off of her lap and retrieved the
book. 'Do you not trust Matteo?'

'No.' Slipping the slim volume under the cushion of my
wingback chair, I rearranged the folds of my dress to cover it
and pasted a smile on my face. 'But I can handle him.'

Paula ushered Georgiana to the door and swung it open to
reveal Matteo and another man – young and slim, wearing a
police uniform. As Paula gestured for them to enter, both men
made a small bow to her and moved in my direction.

'I was just about to make tea,' Paula said, keeping her
daughter close. 'Both of you are welcome to stay, of course.'

'*Grazie, Signora.*' Matteo gestured for the police officer to
proceed ahead of him, and they both halted near my chair.
Paula disappeared into the kitchen with Georgiana to make
tea – and, no doubt, send word to Raphael that Matteo had
arrived with the *polizia*.

'Please take a seat.' I pointed at the sofa, which Paula had
just vacated. 'How may I help you?'

Matteo adjusted his jacket sleeves, then hooked his thumbs
around the narrow lapels in a solemn yet slightly pompous
manner. 'This is our chief of police – Lieutenant Baldini. He
called at my villa today to let me know that a parishioner in
Father Gianni's church has been detained for questioning over
the murder – an evil man who had some long-standing vendetta
with our dear priest. As soon as Lieutenant Baldini informed
me, I wanted him to tell you in person; his deputies are questioning the suspect this very minute, so your mind can be at
rest that the killer will be charged shortly.'

'How kind to think of my well-being,' I murmured,
thinking very rapidly as my glance shifted from one man to
the other. Matteo beamed in satisfaction; Baldini seemed
much less pleased – almost cautious. Had there been a
vendetta at the Basilica di San Lorenzo? Rather fitting that

it would be connected to the church built by the Medicis, but I had never heard Father Gianni mention a blood feud with a member of his parish. Surely he would have mentioned it to me since we were such old friends. 'May I ask the identity of this suspect?'

Baldini shook his head. 'I am afraid that we cannot reveal his name, except to say he is from an old Florentine family that has fallen on hard times. It may be one of the motivations of the attack – this man apparently wanted to take back a priceless gold chalice that his family donated to the church over a hundred years ago, and Father Gianni refused. From all accounts, they had several violent arguments over the request, and the suspect threatened the priest publicly.'

'Very unfortunate,' Matteo echoed.

'Indeed. But I am shocked to hear this news since I heard nothing about it.' I spoke slowly, observing the effect of my words on them. 'I have attended mass there almost every day, and no one has ever mentioned the feud, even the most gossipy members of the basilica—'

'We Florentines tend to keep this type of news quiet from expatriates who live in our city,' Matteo said with a touch of self-righteousness in the set of his chin. 'What is the point in sharing such things, except to confirm foreigners' notion that we Italians are too passionate about our beliefs and personal slights?'

Blinking in feigned dismay, I turned to Matteo. 'I hope you are not referring to me? I consider myself, after all these years, practically a Florentine myself, and I would never be so narrow-minded as to sit in judgment over locals.'

'No, no. Of course not,' Matteo readily agreed, but I thought I detected a skeptical note in his quick assurance. 'But not all visitors are as cosmopolitan as you, my dear Signora Clairmont.'

I acknowledged the compliment with a small nod. 'Let us hope that the killer is swiftly brought to justice and we can put this matter behind us.'

Both men uttered a '*si*' – right at the moment Paula brought in a tray with the teapot and four china cups – and our conversation switched to an upcoming opera performance of Verdi's

Aida that would be held in the nearby Pitti Palace. As they discussed the singers and staging issues, I sat back and quietly sipped my tea. The conversation had turned congenial after the news of a suspect in Father Gianni's death, but something felt slightly off, almost as if I were watching them in a distant reflection that distorted their images. Faces that seemed elongated. Figures that appeared too tall and thin. Flickering light and shadow.

In my heart, I knew that Father Gianni's death had something to do with me – a notion which caused such pain that I could scarcely think about it. I would never have brought him into this situation if I had not been desperate to find the truth. He was with God now, but that was scant consolation.

'Signora, will you be attending the opera performance tomorrow evening?' Matteo was saying.

Blinking, I tried to clear my thoughts. 'In spite of recent events, I would not miss it for the world. Verdi's operas are exquisite in every way – and I expect *Aida* will contain his usual themes of passionate love, betrayal and conspiracy. What more could one expect in a single evening?'

Matteo's features tightened for an instant. 'I hope you do not speak from experience, Signora Clairmont?'

I set my teacup in the saucer with a tiny clatter. 'I cannot speak to betrayal and conspiracy, but with regard to love, I can say that I have some experience, though perhaps my failing memory deceives me about my youthful indiscretions.'

Paula stifled a giggle and Baldini erupted with a short, loud laugh. But Matteo did not seem amused.

'Pardon my frankness,' I followed up with a wink at my niece.

'You are a remarkable woman,' Matteo said as he rose to his feet. He kissed my hand, clasping my fingers with a grip that seemed unnaturally tight. 'Be careful that you do not overtax your strength, Signora Clairmont, since some . . . exertions can cause unnecessary consequences for a woman of your age. You should be enjoying this stage of your life – no distressing upsets or delving into matters that can cause you further anxiety, especially with regard to this matter of

Father Gianni's death. Adopt our *che sarà sarà* attitude. It is much healthier in the long run.'

'Excellent advice,' I said, slowing withdrawing my hand.

As Paula showed the two men out, I set my teacup on the tray and then used the napkin to wipe off my hand where he had touched my fingers. I would leave no trace of Matteo on my skin. His words held kindness, but perhaps an implicit threat? Was he just being cautious or hiding something about Father Gianni's death that he did not want me to find out? Either way, his words conveyed a meaning that I did not like. I might have mellowed slightly in my old age, but I still did not like being told what to do by a man. Certainly, Florentines could be rather secretive about the long-standing vendettas that threaded through the generations, but, as Father Gianni's friend, I deserved to know the truth.

If I had inadvertently precipitated my old friend's demise, I needed to know that as well – to protect Paula and Georgiana.

And no matter what, I was still my own woman and would accomplish this task in my own way and manner.

That evening, I resumed my reading of Polidori's journal and found myself struggling to stay awake. Certainly, my emotional memories of those late-summer days were colored by the passage of time and knowledge of what was to come afterwards, but Polidori's entries made our lives seem trivial. No descriptions of the powerful thunderstorms rolling in from the Alps. No recordings of the conversations at the Villa Diodati when we listened avidly to Byron and Shelley argue about politics. No comments about our ghost stories being recited late at night.

Nothing interesting at all.

Only details about Polidori's interactions with gardeners or disputes with cooks over ill-prepared food at Diodati. Could he have focused on anything more trivial? I now understood why his novel, *The Vampyre*, never found a huge audience. I had never read it, and did not intend to after perusing this tedious narrative.

Scanning the pages rapidly, I was ready to flip the journal shut when I spied a couple of sentences near the bottom that had been marked through with a bold stroke of the pen:

~~August 2nd~~
   ~~Saw Mary today with di Breme at Maison Chapuis~~
~~and talked at length about L.B. and his latest predicament.~~
~~Nothing to be done but eliminate the problem—it has~~
~~grave consequences.~~

Quickly, I sat up and read the lines over. What predicament? I did not remember Mary mentioning that she had met with Polidori on that day, nor did I recall any problem that had cropped up for Byron – aside from my pregnancy. And why was Ludovico di Breme with them? He was the Italian visitor who had dropped by the Villa Diodati to meet Byron during the previous month. I had met him only briefly and heard he had returned to Italy; I never saw him again.

But apparently Mary had – a fact she chose not to share with me.

August 2. That was the day that Shelley and I visited Byron at Diodati to discuss Allegra's future. While Byron paced back and forth across the parlor, Shelley had proposed a financial and visitation plan that was surprisingly practical. Byron would provide a home for the child, along with monetary support, but I would be allowed to visit and exercise my maternal rights. Often, during the discussion, I felt tears run down my cheeks, but I said nothing as I wiped them away, deferring to Shelley in this matter.

Byron had agreed to everything with no objections but, also, no great reluctance. I had expected more, though I knew all my passionate dreams of our having a life together had evaporated into dust. We would never have that type of permanent connection, even though I knew he had cared deeply about me. He was married. Famous. And reconciled to move on. Some of his London friends had traveled to Geneva to see him and they were now pulling his interests in other directions, away from our little group that told ghost stories by candlelight. Our time together was drawing to a close.

But as Byron, Shelley and I had met at Diodati, Mary was entertaining Polidori and di Breme at Maison Chapuis.

Odd that their meeting had been so secret.

Slowly, I turned the page in Polidori's journal to see what he had jotted down next about this secret gathering at Maison Chapuis, and I noticed the top half of the next page had been torn off. I fanned through the last twenty pages to see if it had been inserted somewhere, but nothing showed up.

I flipped to the page with the missing piece again and scrutinized it carefully. The lower section had yet another typical Polidori entry about his horse throwing a shoe. Little help there.

Sitting back against my pillow, I sighed deeply. The more I learned, the less I seemed to really know about that time in my life. Perhaps my memories were so misshapen at this point that I would never really know the truth. Most everyone from my youth was dead, so I had no one else to ask. I had only my recollections . . . and Polidori's journal, however distorted by his depressed mental state.

Did the missing piece hold the key to something related to Allegra? The notation about Byron's 'predicament' seemed to indicate that he had been discussing my pregnancy with Mary and possibly Signor di Breme, though I still could not figure out why *he* was there. The only person who might be able to explain the entry was Mr Rossetti. At the very least, I needed to know if he had that section of the journal. He wanted to purchase my letters, which was a perfect pretext for setting up a meeting with him to inquire about the journal page.

As I lowered the volume to my lap, I began to plot. I had something that Mr Rossetti wanted, and now he might have something that I wanted. More secrets?

As the nearby candle flickered and burned into the night, I sent up a prayer to Father Gianni that I would have the strength to see this whole thing through.

Gloria al Padre
e al Figlio
e allo Spirito Santo.

I prayed to the glory of God, and the spirit of Father Gianni, and to the angelic memory of my daughter.

For ever and ever.

Captain Parker's Log
April 12, 1815
Mount Tambora

We approached Tambora from the east, carefully navigating the Fortuna *along the island coast and around a reef that stretched the length of Sumbawa. High noon, but no light. Hushed and quiet, as though all hope had left this part of the world, never to return.*

The air tasted of powder and dust, and the heat had become even more intense.

Soul-searing.

Mountain of Fire.

The wind kept shifting, so we constantly adjusted the sails to catch the offshore breeze, relying mostly on our mainsail to keep a westward tack. The hull creaked and groaned in the rough, heaving waves, slicing through what we thought was thick seaweed, but it turned out to be a thick, floating mass of dead fish coated with burnt cinders.

Not a good omen.

We left the town of Bima earlier this morning. Was it only two days ago that waves had surged on to the shore after the volcanic eruption, swamping fishing boats and flooding homes? The Kincaids' house on the bluff had survived and, after the waters withdrew, we surveyed what was left of the town and attended to those who had lost their dwellings. People wept as they stood on the foundation of their homes, their lives forever changed.

Before we raised anchor, I took my leave of Kincaid and his wife, knowing it would be a long time before I saw them again.

We did not dare delay since any survivors of Mount Tambora would need our help. In spite of my crew's nervousness, to a man they focused on keeping the Fortuna *on course. No space for mistakes and no time for fear.*

As we steered around a large floating clump of ash near the westernmost tip of Sumbawa, I jerked the rudder with a hard swing to port. The Fortuna *responded with an agile turn, slicing through the heavy, rolling waters with a smooth gliding movement. My men rushed to the portside of the ship to see Tambora and uttered a collective gasp at the sight as our ship drew near. I, too, could hardly take in what lay before me.*

The entire top section of the mountain was gone.

Vanished.

It appeared as if a huge fist had pummeled the mountain's summit, causing a large crater in the center that was several miles wide, with lava flows streaming out of the gaping center and down the mountainside. Floating layers of ash lingered around what was left of Tambora's summit in an immense cloud that stretched high above the jagged peak, as far upward as the eye could see. It seemed to reach into the heavens, though there was nothing divine about what had happened here.

My crew began to murmur prayers in various languages, and I found myself appealing to God in his mercy to spare those who might have survived the eruption. Yet I knew in my heart that it was not possible for anyone to live through such destruction. If the volcanic blast had not instantly killed nearby residents, the lava and ash would most certainly have caused their eventual demise.

I scanned the lower part of Tambora and saw flames shooting out from the sides like fiery spears, stabbing into the air with thin, red shoots.

The Mountain had turned to fire.

And everywhere around the base stretched layers of ash and pumice – no village, no people, no wildlife.

Nothing but the smell of burning death.

Silence descended over us as we sailed past the crumbling mountain and devastated landscape, noting the black masses of pumice stone and the charred, skeletal remains of tree trunks. There was little point in trying to find a safe harbor or hunt for survivors. Instead, I ordered the crew to head south.

If we were lucky, we might find someone still alive.

EIGHT

Geneva, Switzerland, August 28, 1816

Slowly, I ambled through the empty rooms of Maison Chapuis, my footsteps clattering on the cold, hard wood floor. Mary had already packed up all of our household items; Shelley had ordered the furniture to be removed and sent on to Bath, England, in the West Country where the three of us would reside, far from my mother and stepfather's observant eye. They would, no doubt, immediately discern that I was to have a child were they to see me, and I could not bear their constant nagging as to the father's identity.

No, it was best to give birth in secret – not that it would remain so for long. Certainly, nothing in life could be hidden from one's parents for too long; indeed, I think they had already surmised my condition from their letters. The gossip mongering had probably stretched all the way from Geneva to London, with visitors eager to relate my scandalous activities.

In truth, my heart was broken – shattered into so many pieces that I feared I would never be whole again.

A sad affair.

As I stood near the parlor window and gazed up the hill at the Villa Diodati where we had shared so many happy evenings during the summer, I felt a sob rise up in my throat. Never again would the four of us share such a time together – full of excitement and passion and creative fire. I could see it all passing out of my life like a fading echo, already losing some of its sweet magic.

But I regretted nothing.

My hand covered my stomach, feeling the presence of new life, and the sadness shifted into a sense of joy. How could I feel remorse over the creation of a child of love? My mouth curved into a smile as I imagined being a mother, embracing my own child – not Mary's but *mine*. I would live for another being for the first time in my life – a responsibility that I did not take lightly and one that I welcomed heart and soul.

Not only had I experienced the heights and depths of love during this summer, but I had also grown up and learned that no matter how much I wanted something to happen, it just might elude my best attempts. I could not make Byron care for me with the same depth of feeling that I possessed for him, and yet I still trusted in the power of love to raise one above the trivialities of everyday life. I would always believe that reaching for my heart's desire had been the most noble of actions – and the bravest.

Sliding on to the window seat, I touched the glass, tracing the outline of Diodati in the distance, including the high roof and porticoed pillars. Ironically, the storms had finally cleared and the sun peeped out from behind the thick layer of clouds with a bright radiance that I had not seen in months.

I gave a short laugh. Fate truly loved a jest.

Then I heard a familiar footfall: the tap of a boot and sliding drag of the heel across the floor. It grew closer . . . and I turned my head toward the door just at the moment Byron appeared.

He bore the same sad, tired look that I had seen that first day when we encountered each other by Lake Geneva in early summer, almost a lifetime ago. Still wearing his riding breeches and a loose open shirt, he managed to look both elegant and dashing as he paused in the doorway, clutching his riding crop in one hand. In spite of myself, I felt that familiar dance of excitement inside at his magnetic presence.

The silence stretched between us, tense and awkward.

'I could have made you happy, if you had allowed me into your heart,' I finally spoke up in a quiet voice.

'My heart?' He sighed, keeping his gaze averted. 'It is a twisted, barren land – not a place for someone who is so young and full of hope. No, Claire, I would have made you very unhappy, turning that love you feel for me to hate before very long. You are seventeen, and I am almost thirty with a wife and a disgraced past behind me. I have nothing to offer you. Eventually, we would have parted in such bitterness that there would be nothing left for our child.'

'You do not know that,' I protested.

'But I do.' Tossing the riding crop aside, he moved into the empty room with halting steps, his limp more pronounced than ever. 'Look what a chaotic mess I have made of my life. Everyone whom I have loved has either deserted or disowned me. I can never go back to England because of the scandals; I know that now. I will be ostracized for the rest of my days. Can you truly say that is the kind of life you want? You know what it was like here with tourists peering at us through spyglasses and residents cutting us out of the best society—'

'I don't care about any of that!' I rose to my feet and reached out to him. 'Why should it ever end? Why?' I heard the note of desperation in my voice but I did not care. I was fighting for my future.

He moved closer and twisted one dark curl of my hair around his finger. 'You are truly one of Beauty's daughters, are you not?' He asked the question as if he were speaking to himself. 'Your eyes hold the mysteries of foreign lands – full of passion and fire. I could almost lose myself in those eyes.' He lowered his face to mine and I awaited his kiss, already feeling his lips on mine. But he kissed my forehead, not my lips.

My eyelids fluttered open and I saw the truth in his face: it was the kiss of goodbye.

Dropping my arms in defeat, I turned around so he could not see the tears that had welled up. 'You are pushing me away because I am not Mary – my lovely, accomplished step-sister, the woman that every man wants. If I were more like her, you would not let me leave, would you?' I choked back a bitter sob.

'That is not true.' He grasped my upper arms and I felt his breath against the back of my neck. 'Mary is a unique woman, worthy of Shelley in every way, but I have never spent one moment thinking about her in that way—'

'Not ever?'

'No.' He drew me against him and I inhaled the scent of his cologne – a deep, spicy fragrance. 'You are my last great passion, Claire, and I have no desire for another. That part of my life is over now.'

'I can scarcely believe that.' I could not resist adding with some irony, 'After I return to England, I am sure you will not lack female companionship – Polidori will no doubt help in that regard. He has always hated me and will be only too happy to find future replacements.' As I spoke the words, I knew they sounded churlish, but part of me believed that Polidori had tried to undermine my influence over Byron – perhaps even to the point of doing me harm.

Slowly, he turned me in his arms. 'That is not true. You ascribe power to him that he does not possess. He is but a silly young man – and, in truth, I do not intend to keep him in my employ for long after we leave Geneva. I have tired of his fits of temper. But I have never heard him utter a word of criticism about you in my presence.'

'But at Chillon—'

'You slipped on the steps.' He held my gaze steadily. 'Mary told me that you thought someone might have pushed you, but is that likely?'

I hesitated. Mary should not have shared my suspicions.

'No one knew you had traveled to Chillon to meet Shelley and me, so how it is possible that an attacker lay in wait for your appearance at the castle?' Trailing his fingers across my cheek, his touch seemed almost tender. 'After that hellish two-day trip by land . . . in your condition . . . you had to be exhausted. You fell and had a fever that caused you to rave for days. I do not blame you for imagining all kinds of things – even attempted murder.'

I bit my lip. My suspicions sounded foolish when stated so starkly: the silly fantasies of a pregnant woman in an uncertain situation. I just did not know anymore.

'The only thing that matters is that you and the child are safe and healthy. You will return to England, have the baby, and I will honor all of my promises—'

'What if it is a boy? Would you feel differently about our future together if I bore you a son?' I searched his face – so familiar and so dear to me, waiting for a change of heart. But he merely shook his head. 'Shelley left his wife for Mary,' I continued, 'and he is constantly trying to make their son, William, his heir, though Shelley's father opposes it vehemently.'

'But that is his father's decision; it is his estate, and Shelley's reputation is tarnished, as is mine. No, his father will never relent as long as Shelley's wife still lives. I know these aristocrats – they do not allow others into their sacred circles if they can help it. And you know our child could never inherit my estate; it will go to my legitimate daughter with my wife. Even if we divorce in the course of time, I will no doubt have to concede my wife's dowry that she brought to the marriage and acknowledge Ada as my heir. It is not to say that I cannot provide for *our* child, no matter the sex, but . . .' His words trailed off. *Our child would be illegitimate.*

It was a cruel world. I never knew my father, and now my child would never know the respectability of having a family.

Looking down, I murmured, 'I understand.' And I truly did at this point. There was little reason to keep pressing for a future that would never happen.

He tipped up my chin. 'You will have Shelley and Mary to support you in your confinement and beyond, never fear. Shelley is a gentleman, one of the best souls that I have ever known, and he can always be counted on for the honorable course. He is, in fact, a better man than I – in every way.'

I did not respond.

Frowning, Byron's eyes took on a shadow of guilt. 'I have disappointed you, my dear – and for that I am sorry. If I could go back in time to when we met in England, I would have behaved very differently and been more prudent about starting a relationship when my life was crumbling around me. It should never have happened—'

'No!' Jerking back from him, I uttered the word yet again, even more emphatically. 'I will never lament our relationship, or our child. *Ever.*'

A smile appeared on his face. 'What I could accomplish still in this world if I had your conviction, my dear. I envy you that above all things.'

'So you are to be your hero, Childe Harold, after all? "Grown aged in this world of woe"?' I quoted.

Wincing as I recited the lines from the third canto of his poem, he then shrugged. 'It appears that will be my fate.'

'Such a melancholy thought.' Slipping on to the window seat again, I felt my emotions drain away like the air emptying from a balloon – a long, drawn-out deflation. 'You will miss my fair copies of your poems . . .'

'I will miss much about you, Claire, though your hand-writing is probably not at the top of my list.' Amusement flickered across his face as he gave a rueful laugh.

I managed a smile.

'Never question your charms . . . they are considerable.' After a few moments, he bent down awkwardly and retrieved the riding crop, then straightened again.

Folding my hands in my lap, I felt our time drawing to a close. 'Where do you intend to go next?'

'I am not certain. My dear friend, Hobhouse, should arrive soon, and he wants to travel to the Jungfrau and then see Mount Blanc. I shall play the tourist again.'

'And after that?' Glancing out of the window once more, I took one last look at the majestic outlines of the Villa Diodati. The beautiful arches and graceful awning. A gem perched on the lakeshore. 'What then?'

Rapping his riding crop against the black leather boot that encased his clubfoot, he stared at the floor. 'Perhaps south to Italy. I have heard that a man can lose himself in the decadent world of Venice on the Grand Canal, and that sounds appealing right now. No more philosophizing. Just sensual pleasure to make a man forget.'

I shuddered inwardly.

'Since I can never return to England, what does it matter?' He gave the boot a hard strike. 'Hell and damnation. Claire, why do you not come—'

'My lord, your horse awaits,' Polidori cut in as he hurried into the room. He wore almost the same riding clothing as Byron, except he sported an elaborate cravat around his neck. 'I believe you have an engagement and you are overdue.'

Do not leave, my love.

Was Byron about to ask me to go to Italy with him? My

hands curled into fists and I began to rise in protest at Polidori's interruption.

But Byron gave a curt nod to his physician. 'Yes, I must take my leave of you, Claire . . . Take care, my dear.'

'Shall we meet again?' I said in a choking voice.

He lingered for a few seconds, then, without another word, exited the room, drawing all of the light from my world.

He was gone.

My head sagged in defeat. It was over. Byron did not need to say anything because I knew that I would never see him again.

When I looked up, I felt the venom in my glare directed at Polidori. 'You poisoned him against me, and I do not understand why. I never did anything to cause your dislike except love him. Perhaps that is what caused it; you did not want to share him with me.'

'Do not be ridiculous,' he responded in a quiet voice as he moved to the center of the room. 'I never bore you any ill will, nor am I jealous of Byron's . . . acquaintances. Do you really think I do not see him for who he is? The Great Poet!' he scoffed. 'Oh, no one can deny he is a genius, but he is also a self-absorbed aristocrat who sees everyone as merely a bit player in the drama of his life. I have watched him treat people with the utmost carelessness, and I have been disgusted.'

I sat back, stunned at his diatribe. He had rarely spoken more than a handful of words to me, and now he was waxing bitter about the man whom we all idolized. Not that I disagreed. I, too, had seen that side of Byron and found myself dismayed, but who among us is not self-serving in some manner?

'You seem surprised, but I am not as easily swayed as you may have thought. Indeed, I am more than capable of forming my own views about Byron, even if he is my employer.'

'I . . . I do not know what to say, except that all signs during the entire summer conveyed the impression that you do, in fact, dislike me.'

He paused. 'That is far from the truth. Ask Mary. I never spoke ill of you to her or anyone else – not even when I guessed your secret before you told Byron.' He looked deliberately at my stomach. 'And I never revealed my suspicions to him, either. It was for you to tell him.'

Instinctively, my hands moved there in a protective shield. 'How did you know so quickly?'

He raised one brow. 'We "bit players" often notice what others do not see.'

Taking in his words, my mind reeled with confusion. Polidori *seemed* sincere enough, but his past behavior had done nothing to earn my confidence. Quite the opposite. 'Why did you take so long to reveal yourself?'

'I have my reasons.'

'And my every instinct tells me that you are false,' I exclaimed. 'Especially after the incident at Chillon—'

'You are wrong to think me such a villain.'

Rising to my feet, I watched him with a critical squint. 'You did not push me down the stairs?'

'No.'

As I took in his firm response, I felt as if my world had shifted slightly. Had I been wrong about him? I could not answer for certain at this point.

'No more, please.' I covered my face, blotting him out as I tried to quieten my chaotic thoughts. 'I cannot bear to hear anything else right now.' Once I had time to accept that the love of my life had parted from me forever, maybe I could begin to consider that I had been in error about Polidori's role in our lives. It was a remote possibility – and one that, for now, I could not accept.

Polidori gently eased my hands away from my face. 'You are going back to England and I am traveling to Italy with Byron, so it hardly matters what you think of me since we shall never see each other again. But I did not want you to leave still having the wrong idea of my motivations.'

Raising my chin in polite skepticism, I continued, 'I cannot *thank* you, if that is what you seek. Too much has passed between us.'

His face shuttered down.

'We leave tomorrow, so I will bid you farewell.' I extended my hand.

Ignoring the gesture, he leaned forward and whispered in

my ear. 'Do not have this child – it will bring you only heartache.'

Taking in a sharp breath, I immediately jerked back. 'How dare you say that to me? I should have known that I was right about you . . . Only a hateful, vile man could suggest such a thing. Get out of my sight.'

His jaw clenched. 'You will see that I was right.' He turned on his heel and strode out of the room.

Standing in the deserted, empty room for a long moment, I felt a firm sense of resolve rise up inside me. My perceptions about Polidori *had* been correct. He was my enemy who had worked against me. A reprehensible man. But it hardly mattered now that my relationship with Byron was over.

Once I was back in England with Mary and Shelley, I would have my baby and Geneva would be nothing but a memory.

A new chapter in my life was about to begin.

Captain Parker's Log
April 14, 1815
Mount Tambora

We have been looking for survivors for two days now.

Once we sailed the Fortuna *south of the smoke and fire of Mount Tambora, the air began to clear; a dim, watery sun appeared in the sky. We still wore cotton scarfs tied around our lower faces because of the gritty particles that lingered in the air, but we breathed more easily.*

As our ship paralleled the west coast of Sumbawa toward the Bay of Saleh, we anxiously scanned the shore for any survivor who might have escaped the eruption. I wanted to close my eyes and never see such sights again, but they seemed to burn into my eyes. Dead fish floating in the water. Dead cattle on the beaches. Skeletal trees, not just stripped of bark but incinerated into ashen forms. Nothing remained.

Either the villagers who lived at the base of Mount Tambora had not escaped in time to avoid the gasses and lava flow, or they had moved into the mountainous interior beyond our vision, but we saw no living being.

My men did not speak much; they simply adjusted the

*sails and kept hunting the beach. We all knew that death
had come to this part of the world in a violent, cataclysmic
eruption, and life here would never be the same.*

I *would never be the same.*

*All these months, I had driven my crew to take on
larger cargos so we could make more wealth than we had
ever deemed possible, and we all stood to profit hugely
from our labors. On this – our last voyage – we had
expected to bring in so much money that we could all
return to England as well-to-do men. The dream of wealth
and power had driven us all.*

*And now the vanity of my own desires seemed so feeble
as we beheld the Mountain of Fire's power.*

Man was nothing in the face of such destruction.

I *was nothing.*

*Just then, I heard one of my men yell out, 'There – I
see someone!'*

*Shading my eyes with my hand, I squinted to make out
what he was pointing at on the shore, but I could not see
a shape or form in the distance. I blinked a few times to
clear my vision and then I saw a woman waving her
hands above her head. She wore a dirty, tattered sarong
and had long, dark hair covered in gray ash. A large
group of children emerged from the blasted trees beyond
her, followed by elderly women, all of them screaming
and motioning for us to come ashore.*

'Survivors!' I shouted.

My first mate dashed to the Fortuna*'s bow with two
other crewmen. In minutes, they had lowered the anchor
and dropped the sails. Once he returned, I instructed him
to lower the three skiffs that we could row in close enough
to pick up the women and children who were stranded
on the beach.*

*'Captain, we do not have room in our cargo hold for
all of them,' my first mate said, glancing back at the
survivors. 'There must be a hundred of them, and our
hold is filled to capacity with the spices, silks and
tea . . .'*

The crew halted in their frantic efforts to break out

the small boats and gathered into a close circle around me.

I cleared my throat. 'You heard the first mate. We do not have room for the large number of survivors and, though we could probably take most of the children, we will have the leave the women behind.' I paused. 'As your captain, I could order you to bring all of them on to our ship, but I will not do that. You worked hard for this cargo, and I cannot ask you to empty out the hold and lose everything. It has to be your decision, and I will abide by it.'

They exchanged glances, faces drawn tight with uncertainty. Then my first mate pulled out a small packet of tea . . . and threw it into the water. One by one, the rest of the crew followed with their individual tea caches.

'All right, men, let's get those boats to shore . . . and empty out the hold, except for the food. They have probably seen no food for two days and will be close to starving by the time they arrive on board.' I motioned for half of the crew to lower the skiffs, while the other men disappeared below deck. In a short time, the small boats headed for the beach and my crew began heaving large barrels of tea and spices into the sea. The wood split open upon impact on the water's surface, causing a trail of green and black tea to spill out and snake out into the undercurrent.

As I watched this spectacle, something odd took place within me. I began to feel lighter – almost weightless – as if a great burden had been lifted from me.

I now had a more important task before me than making my fortune.

And I would not fail.

NINE

Florence, Italy, 1873

Opera night had arrived.

I stood in front of the full-length gilt mirror in my bedroom and looked long and hard at the image that was reflected back at me in the late-afternoon light. Long, black lace dress that fell in elegant (if slightly shabby) folds to my ankles, with my mother's gold locket at my throat. Graying hair upswept into an elaborate style. A face that seemed (at least to me) to still hold a glimpse of my youth in the sparkle of my dark eyes. Perhaps I deceived myself, but at seventy-five it was my right to do so. I preferred to think of myself as a woman who still had one great adventure left in her life.

Maybe even my most important adventure yet.

I intended to solve the great mystery of my life: what had happened to my daughter, Allegra. For whatever reason these events had unfolded in Florence during the last week, I did not really care, except to know that I would see this journey through to the end and find the answers that I have always sought.

As I stared at the reflection of my aging face, I saw the young version of myself – so vibrant and eager, wanting to pursue love with a reckless passion. I saw the joyful mother turned grieving parent. I saw the middle-aged, restless woman who traveled incessantly to avoid having a permanent home. I saw the doting aunt who loved her relatives and finally found peace in an Italian city that had been the place of many of her happiest times.

So many memories.

And through it all, I tried never to lose my zest for life, no matter what. I would never lose that verve until the day I died, which would not be for a little while yet since I now had unfinished business in *this* world.

'Aunt Claire, are you ready?' Paula entered my room, Georgiana in hand. My niece had donned her best (and only) evening dress of soft white silk with tiny embroidered rose buds and a low-cut bodice. Her blond waves were caught up in a loose chignon threaded with fresh flowers – her favorite inexpensive adornment. In contrast, Georgiana still wore her gingham play dress and a mischievous grin.

'You look lovely, my dear Paula.' I extended my hands; she took one and her daughter took the other.

'Do not leave me here,' Georgiana whined, burying her face in my skirt. 'I want to go, too – and see the opera.'

'I know, but we will be out late and little girls need their sleep.' Smoothing down her curls, I murmured some words of endearment in Italian to soothe her, even as I exchanged glances with Paula.

'Did you send the message to Mr Rossetti?' I whispered to Paula.

She nodded. 'He will meet us during the intermission of *Aida* in the Boboli Gardens behind the Pitti Palace, near the obelisk.'

'Perfect – there is no better place to do business than a social occasion.' The whole of Florence would be at the palace's performance of Verdi's latest opera, *Aida* – a story set in Egypt about love and loss. It had opened to much acclaim two years before in Cairo, and the Florentines were most excited to watch their beloved Verdi's newest music. Under any other circumstances, I would have been overjoyed to listen to his exquisite arias, but this evening held another purpose: I intended to query Mr Rossetti about Polidori's journal and, I hoped, find the missing part and missing piece of information about that summer of 1816.

Perhaps that part of the journal held the key to why Byron let me leave him and why Polidori had counseled me to abort my own child. If Mr Rossetti did not possess the missing piece, so be it. Then, I would ask about the note under my teacup. It would be my last attempt to find the truth, and I could finally put my suspicions to rest.

'Raphael will accompany us to the Pitti Palace and wait near the obelisk until Mr Rossetti appears,' she continued in a hushed voice.

I squeezed her hand and nodded. It would be only a short distance since our rooms overlooked the Boboli Gardens and the palace was at the opposite end of the cultivated terraces and foliage. My ankle felt strong again, and I could easily walk there with Paula and Raphael.

Taking her daughter's hand again, Paula gently drew her to the front door. 'I will drop Georgiana at Maria's house next door and will meet you out front, Aunt.'

I waved them off. Once they had exited, I picked up Polidori's journal which I had left on the table, and my glance fell on that silver inkwell that Shelley had given to me all those years ago. He and Mary had been my dear and true family – or so I thought.

Slipping the journal into my bag, which already held a small stack of letters, I took one last look at the inkwell . . . then let myself out of our rooms.

Once downstairs, I joined Paula and Raphael – he had donned a neatly pressed white shirt and black trousers, and combed back his thick, dark hair. He made a handsome partner for my niece, and my heart swelled at the sight of them. So young and beautiful. I loved Paula dearly and would accept any man who cared deeply for her . . . as long as he was true to her. I now believed that Raphael was, indeed, true of heart.

We strolled down the Via Romano toward the Pitti Palace, and I noted how the crowds began to cluster at the entrance, all chattering excitedly in Italian. A new opera by Verdi was practically a national event because he was so beloved by one and all. I, too, found myself entranced by the beauty of his music and would have joined in the excitement were it not for the reason of our being here.

Situated on the south side of the Arno River, near the Ponte Vecchio, the palace had a severe and foreboding appearance, with its rusticated stonework and small Romanesque arches. The original builder, a wealthy banker named Luca Pitti, had positioned the palace on a small hill above the city but apparently rejected the fifteenth-century trend of graceful, smooth

Florentine architecture and favored the rough, coarse facade. Eventually, the Medicis bought the palace and made it their residence, but little was done to alter its appearance, except for adding the Boboli Gardens.

Ah, the gardens . . .

Giardino di Boboli.

The exquisite complex of lovely meadows and flowing waters that unfolded behind the palace in a large triangular shape, comprising many acres. A living, breathing experience of delicate fragrances and natural beauty. My favorite places were the hidden grottos and Roman statues that ringed the fountains. And, of course, the obelisk.

A man in seventeenth-century dress appeared at the massive front doors of the palace and rang a bell. *'Buona sera . . . buona sera. Entrare.'* He gestured for the crowd to enter, and they pressed forward, carrying us along in the wave of humanity. We moved through the doors and found a large temporary theater that had been set up in the *cortile* – the immense interior court with a high-domed ceiling that could hold hundreds of people.

Paula and Raphael quickly found chairs for us near the farthest wall which held a series of round, arched windows. The slanted early-evening light came streaming into the room, causing the temperature to feel even warmer.

'It is stifling in here.' I snapped open my fan and tried to cool myself as I sat down. 'Do you see Mr Rossetti here?' Scanning the audience as they took their seats, I nodded to a few acquaintances, both Italian and English, and received the usual polite smiles. They were all dressed in their finest, which was far more elegant than our own well-worn evening attire.

The two violinists in the small orchestra began to tune their instruments.

'I do not see Rossetti anywhere.' Paula remained on her feet, trying to see over the audience members' heads.

'Va bene,' Raphael said, urging her to sit.

With one last look around the room, Paula took her seat.

Not long after, the first chord of *Aida* began and, in spite of myself, I was transfixed by the performance. The Egyptian scenery had a flat, wooden feel – this was not La Scala with its elaborate sets – but the arias soared with powerfully emotional notes. *Celeste Aida.* The beautiful song sung by Radames transported me into the world of their undying love:

Un regal serto sul crin posarti,
Ergerti un trono vicino al sol, ah!
I'll place a royal wreath upon your crown,
and build you a throne close to the sun!

Closing my eyes, I let the opera lyrics swirl around me in an eddy of joy, despair and sorrow. *Ah, the melodrama.* Some of the audience openly wept at the moment when the Egyptian king betrothed his son, Radames, to Aida, promising that the two of them will be together forever . . .

Act II, Scene II ended and the intermission began. Taking our cue, Paula and I rose and headed toward the rear exit that led to the gardens. Raphael accompanied us to the door, then kissed Paula on the cheek and disappeared into the crowd.

We paused at the threshold. 'Are you ready?' I asked my niece.

'Yes.' She linked her arm through mine and, with slow and deliberate steps, we headed outside into the growing twilight. Immediately, I inhaled the scent of jasmine – a deep and pungent fragrance that seemed to grow stronger as the daylight faded.

Not knowing what would come of our meeting with Mr Rossetti, we could only trust in Providence.

Twenty minutes later, Paula and I stood in the amphitheater, near the obelisk, tapping our toes with impatience. The large, open space, ringed with oak trees and Roman sculptures, was now deserted, but Mr Rossetti still had not arrived. Surely, he could not have missed the obelisk. The huge, needle-shaped structure was unmistakable; it stretched over fifteen feet high. Brought to the Boboli Gardens in 1790 from the Medicis' villa in Rome, the obelisk had been placed at the center of the amphitheater and remained as a symbol of the family's power and position in Florence.

'Do you think he had second thoughts about meeting us?' Paula inquired, pulling her embroidered shawl over her shoulders. The sun had already dipped below the horizon and a tiny chill had entered the air.

'Perhaps, though my note said that I wanted only to return the journal and discuss the sale of my letters – nothing more.' I retrieved Polidori's book of jottings from my bag and flipped through it, stopping at the place part of a page had been ripped out. 'Rossetti will want the journal back, I am sure of it.'

'Indeed, I do,' a now-familiar voice said from behind us.

We both turned and I greeted Mr Rossetti, dressed in an immaculate evening suit, with pleasantries. 'Did you see the first two acts of *Aida*? We could not find you in the cortile.'

'No, I am afraid that I was detained over an Italian drawing that I wanted dearly.' He looked up at the obelisk and gave a whistle of appreciation. 'I have never seen this particular object before – it is remarkable. Egyptian, yes?'

'Of course. I believe it originated from the Temple of the Sun God in 1200 B.C. The Romans brought it to Italy, and the Medicis somehow acquired it like so many other priceless artifacts,' I mused.

He laughed. 'Everything is for sale, is it not?'

I did not respond; instead, I held up the book. 'Thank you for allowing me to read Polidori's journal . . . it was most enlightening to remember the fine details of our life during that summer in Geneva. He had quite the eye for . . . minutiae.'

'Most diplomatic, Miss Clairmont,' he said as he traced the hieroglyphic letters carved into the obelisk. 'Let us be honest: my uncle was not exactly a great chronicler of the famous people he knew, but I believe I can edit the work to make it more palatable to the English reading public. At least, I hope so.'

Smiling, I handed him the journal. 'I did see something odd last night, though. It is as if part of a page has been deliberately torn out.' I paused and cleared my throat, deciding to be direct. 'Did you remove it?'

Flipping the pages, he shrugged. 'Was there something in particular you wanted to see on that date?'

'Not that I recollect – just curious,' I responded, trying to keep my voice light. It felt like a game of cat and mouse. Was it possible that Mr Rossetti had nothing beyond the actual journal – no secrets about the 'haunted summer,' no clues as

to why Polidori disliked me so much, no new revelations about
Allegra? He was here simply to buy my letters.

Maybe I had let my feverish imagination take me into a
realm of silly suppositions.

Foolish.

'Miss Clairmont, have I offended you?' He tilted his head
and frowned. 'I know I was not completely honest at first
about my relationship with John Polidori, but I thought that
you knew; everything else has been absolutely truthful – please
believe me.'

'I do . . . and I have taken no offense, sir.'

Paula slipped an arm around my shoulders and gave me a
brief hug, no doubt sensing my disappointment.

The frown deepened. 'Do you intend to sell the letters? I
assumed that is why you wanted to meet with me. Do you
have them with you?'

Reaching into my bag, I pulled out the small stack of letters
tied with a black velvet ribbon that Shelley had written to me,
but I had kept out the missives from Byron. I could not part
with them. Ever. Though he had broken my heart, I could not
let him go completely, even after all these years.

A wide grin spread across Mr Rossetti's face. 'There must
be at least fifty letters there.'

'Sixty-two,' I replied, toying with the ribbon.

He then quoted a large sum in lire that he was willing to
pay, which made Paula and me both gasp.

'Truly?' Disbelief threaded through my niece's voice.

'I have never been more certain of anything.' He tucked the
journal under his arm and took the letters from me as if I had
given him a precious gift. 'I will include them in my biography
of Shelley and restore you to your rightful place in his circle
– then, down the road, I will edit my uncle's journal. Your
reputation will be in safe hands; make no mistake. I shall not
mention your daughter.'

'You would do that for me?'

'Indeed, yes.'

Now, it was time for me to agree to his terms. Accept the
money, put the past behind me and ensure that Paula had a
secure future. It was the wise decision.

'And now I have something more to tell you,' he began.
'The torn page—'

'I believe you all have something that belongs to me.' Matteo strolled forward from the other side of the obelisk with a small pistol in his hand.

'Matteo? What are you doing here?' I demanded. 'And what exactly do you think you own of mine?'

He jerked his head in the direction of the letters and then snatched them out of Mr Rossetti's unresisting grasp. 'These *lettere* are mine.'

'They are *not!*' I protested.

'Ah, Signora, I disagree.' He leveled the gun at Paula and I froze. 'Do you think I rented those rooms to you so cheaply out of kindness? Or made sure you had enough food not to starve? Or put up with that whining *bambina*—'

'Georgiana does not whine,' Paula cut in with some indignation.

'*Silencio*,' he hissed. 'I had heard rumours about the famous English poets who wrote to you, and realized those letters would fetch many *lire* on the open market. I waited for you to offer them to me in payment for my many kindnesses, and when that did not happen, I decided to steal them. But you always had them locked away, and I could never gain access to your apartment long enough to rifle through your belongings. In desperation, I was even going to persuade Raphael to pilfer the letters, but he fell in love with your niece, so I dropped that plan.' He pivoted toward Mr Rossetti. 'Until this Englishman appeared, I had lost hope that I would ever obtain them. But when it was rumored around Firenze that you were going to sell the letters to him, I waited for my opportunity to step in . . .'

'You are despicable,' I spat out.

He just laughed.

'I beg of you to leave the ladies alone.' Mr Rossetti spoke up in a calm voice. 'You and I can come to some agreement over the letters and make certain that Miss Clairmont is duly compensated—'

'The noble Englishman? I have no intention of paying her, or you, *anything*. What you do not know is that my family is bankrupt . . . I have no money left because of my gambling, even if I did want to pay for the *lettere*. I have nothing left to lose.' Matteo waved the gun for emphasis, and we all drew back.

'Do you intend to kill us over some letters?' I tried to nudge Paula behind me, but she refused to move.

'Like poor Father Gianni?' he grated out in a harsh tone.

'You murdered him?' I cried out in disbelief. 'That cannot be true.'

'It was an accident.' Matteo bared his teeth in snarl. 'When I was at the basilica, praying for divine intervention over my debts, I saw you hand the priest a letter; I saw that you were trying to enlist his help in obtaining a good price from the Englishman. Father Gianni knew of my desperate financial situation, but when I confronted him the next day in the Old Sacristy, he refused to help me. I tried to take that *lettera* you had given him. We struggled and he fell against the altar . . .' Matteo broke off with a catch in his throat. 'I blame *you*, Signora. It was your fault. You are obsessed with your daughter – the one that died in the convent. I overheard your conversation with Father Gianni about her, but you cannot bring her back, or the *parroco* now. You killed him with your delusions.'

'Not true. I never would have seen him if not for that note about Allegra under my teacup—'

'*Non è vero, Signora.*'

Dear God. I closed my eyes briefly, realizing how wrong I had been about everything, including Father Gianni's death. 'Take the letters then, and go!'

'Aunt Claire, they are *yours*!' Paula protested.

I touched her cheek. 'I do not care anymore . . . they have caused too much grief, my dear.'

Mr Rossetti stepped in front of us. 'We will call the police, you understand.'

'I shall be long gone.' He pocketed the letters and tipped the pistol in a salute. '*Addio.*'

As he turned, Raphael emerged from his position in the hidden grotto and wrestled him to the ground. The pistol fell to the side and Paula immediately snatched it up, screaming for the *polizia* as Raphael and Matteo rolled over and over toward the sharp edge of the obelisk. Paula aimed the pistol upwards and fired at the sky and the fight ceased, as did the music inside the palace.

Two members of the *polizia* raced outside; once they reached us, they pulled Matteo and Raphael apart.

Pointing at Matteo with a shaky hand, I exclaimed, 'Thief! Murderer!'

Paula dropped the pistol and fell to her knees as Mr Rossetti explained in Italian what had happened. By that time, everyone had rushed out of the palace and stood at the courtyard rail, peering at us through the darkness and murmuring in hushed tones.

I bent down and hugged Paula close, both of us trembling.

The nightmare had finally ended – not exactly a last act in the way that I had anticipated, but a finale nonetheless.

I could put all my doubts to rest about Father Gianni's death – and perhaps those about my long-lost daughter, Allegra.

They were both gone.

TEN

'Are you all right, Miss Clairmont?' Mr Rossetti asked me as we stood next to the obelisk. Darkness had fallen, but the *polizia* had left a lantern which provided a tiny glow of light.

'Yes – and no.' I could barely take in that my landlord had just confessed to attempted theft and accidental murder – but, in an odd way, it seemed almost a relief to end the bizarre twist of events over the last week.

And a sad realization that none of it had to do with Allegra's death.

She had died more than fifty years ago. I grieved it then, and I would grieve it now. But I had to accept it.

And poor Father Gianni's death, as well.

Mr Rossetti gave me the letters. 'You never really wanted to sell them, did you?'

'What do you think? Would you barter your past?' I slipped them back into my bag. 'Our poverty drove me to consider it. But I cannot part with them – not now, not ever. I apologize, sir.'

'You have nothing to be sorry for,' he hastened to reassure me. 'I have never experienced such an . . . eventful trip to Italy. And no matter what, I will include you in my biography of Shelley – truthfully and discreetly.'

'You are most generous. I will, of course, allow you to read them.'

'*Grazie.*' He glanced at the obelisk. 'It really is a magnificent structure – I can see why you chose to live nearby.'

'Indeed.'

It was time to go home. Paula and I would have to start planning for the recent downturn of our financial aspirations. At least we knew for certain where Raphael's allegiance lay – if he married Paula, perhaps the three of us, with Georgiana, could find cheaper lodgings.

Sighing, I reached for the lantern to make my way back.

'You know . . . I also find it interesting that a missing part of my uncle's journal was attached to a drawing of this obelisk,' he added.

I halted.

Mr Rossetti reached into his jacket and pulled out a small scroll of parchment. As he unfurled it to reveal an artist's rendering of the obelisk, I noticed the half page from Polidori's journal – with its jagged edge – attached to the back of the drawing.

'You have the missing piece of the page,' I said quietly.

'I was going to tell you when Matteo appeared,' he said. '*I* did not rip it out of the journal – someone else did. When my mother finally agreed to give Polidori's journal to me last year, I noted part of a page had been torn. She recalled that it had been sent to her a few years after his death – attached to this sketch.' He grasped the lantern and held it up to the pen and ink drawing of the obelisk with the words *For Claire – There be none of Beauty's daughters, 1822*, scrawled across one corner.

'That is Byron's writing – I would recognize it anywhere,' I said breathlessly. 'But is it possible that *he* had the missing part of Polidori's journal?'

'I cannot say for certain, except that it, along with the drawing, was sent to my mother anonymously in 1824.'

A sudden realization dawned upon me. 'That was the year Byron died fighting for Greek independence in Missolonghi.'

He nodded. 'My mother recognized the journal entry as belonging to Polidori, so when she had the sketch framed, she simply left it on the back. Eventually, she forgot all about it – until I asked her about the missing section . . . The artist is Giuseppe Cades and his work is quite valuable. I was arranging for it to be sent to you through Trelawny, but he suggested that I travel here to give it to you personally when I inquired about the sale of your correspondence. He also instructed me to place the note under your teacup the day we first met, but made me vow not to read it – I did as he wished.'

'I . . . I do not know what to say.' My thoughts began to spin in a vortex of dazed confusion. Could it be that Byron and Polidori had been in collusion over some nameless deceit?

'From what I could tell last night, the lost entry was from the summer of 1816 when I was already pregnant with Byron's child. I cannot decipher it in this dim light, but does it contain anything startling?'

'That depends on your perspective, I suppose.' He paused as he flipped over the sketch and traced a few lines on the journal fragment. 'A notation, such as this one, that states Byron and Shelley were settling an illegitimate child's future might be seen as scandalous to some. Not to me, of course.' Smiling, he gave me the drawing and missing part of the page. 'Perhaps we could talk about it over tea tomorrow? You could explain what all of this means and, if you are inclined to sell the Cades sketch, I could locate a buyer.'

'I would like to have tea together, but as to selling the artwork, I must consider that carefully.' My gratitude toward him soared. Although the journal entry had provided no great revelations about Allegra, the pen and ink sketch could fetch many *lire* and signal the end of our poverty – should I choose to sell it. It would support Paula and Georgiana in comfort during my last days, and beyond. Perhaps . . .

He remained motionless, then gave a little bow. 'You are truly remarkable, Miss Clairmont. If you would like a few minutes alone, I need to give the police my statement – and will return shortly to see you home. Raphael has already escorted Paula back to your apartment.'

'Thank you.' I clasped the drawing to my chest and nodded.

Once he had left, I glanced down at Giuseppe Cades' rendition of the obelisk again – spear straight – with the lovely, graceful foliage of the Boboli Gardens framing it in bold strokes.

Who had sent this drawing to Mr Rossetti's mother?

Most puzzling.

But I knew *why* Byron had kept this image of the obelisk and inscribed it to me. It was part of *our* past; it was the reason I had chosen to spend my later years near the Boboli Gardens – because this place held a secret, a stolen moment that I had kept hidden from everyone, including Paula.

Setting the lantern to the side of the obelisk, I knelt down and began to dig at the ground with my bare hands. Feeling the dirt beneath my fingers gave me a demonic energy. I kept digging and digging, knowing what lay underneath the earth.

I knew because I had placed it there when I met Byron here, a few months after Allegra's death.

About ten inches under the surface, I felt a box – small and rectangular. Scooping it out, I held it close, remembering the last time I had seen it.

In 1822, six months after Allegra had died, Byron had ridden all night to see me in Florence, and we agreed to meet by the obelisk at sunset . . .

When I saw him limp down the courtyard stairs, I realized that it had been almost seven years since we parted in Geneva. His hair was heavily threaded with gray; he had grown quite thin and pale, dragging his clubfoot with a hard, stiff gait as he leaned on a walking stick.

As he drew near, I felt overcome by emotion – all that we had shared together, and lost.

'My dear Claire.' He kissed my hand, then stood back and surveyed me. 'You look well.'

'As do you,' I lied.

He gave a short laugh. 'Hardly.'

An awkward silence fell over us, then I cleared my throat. 'Shelley told me that you were about to leave Ravenna.'

'Soon.'

'Where do you go next?'

He stared up at the tip of the obelisk and shook his head. 'I do not know. My days rarely seem my own now—'

'With Teresa?' I could not help but mention his Italian mistress; everyone had talked about them since she left her husband for Byron.

'That's over.' He shrugged. 'Mostly, I spend a great deal of time alone or in activities that I should know better than to indulge in . . . but there you have it: I am what I am.'

'Indeed.'

'In truth, I sail for Greece soon to aid the freedom fighters against the Ottomans. Who knows? Perhaps I shall redeem myself by becoming one of my own heroes. But would you believe me if I said how much I cherished that summer in Geneva? Shelley, Mary, you and me – it was a charmed circle.'

'And the most wonderful time of my life,' I murmured.

He leaned in close. 'Truly, I am so sorry for what happened to Allegra. I have been tormented by her loss and by what you must feel. I would not blame you if you hated me.'

Tears spilled down my cheeks. 'I do not hate you.'

'I have something to give you.' He held out a gold and enamel box and opened the lid to reveal a lock of hair attached to a tiny piece of paper with the name *Allegra Byron* written on it. 'The nuns at Bagnacavallo gave it to me after she . . . died. I thought we could bury it here and put our past to rest. We can bury our daughter together.'

I touched the lock and her lovely face rose up in my mind. My sweet daughter.

I turned away and heard him snap the lid shut.

He thumped at the ground with his walking stick, digging at the dirt until he had made a small hole. Then he bent down and placed the box in the little recess and I covered it with the loose soil.

The task was done.

We then stood up and faced each other.

'Promise me, Claire, that you will never look at the box again – or grieve for our daughter endlessly,' he said quietly. 'You have many years ahead of you, I think, and you must not lose that love of life that so entranced me.'

'I will honor your first request, but as to not grieving for the rest of my years, I cannot vow to that.'

'I will not forget you.' He touched his cheek to mine; his was cold. 'When I am gone, remember what we buried here.'

The words caught in my throat, and I could not answer him – just watch him leave me for the second time in my life.

'Goodbye, my love,' I whispered before he disappeared into the shadows . . .

Blinking back the tears, I came back into the present.

My hands shook as I eased open the ornately gilded enamel lid. Inside still lay the lock of Allegra's hair – a tiny blonde curl that made me smile.

My beloved daughter.

I would carry it with me now. There was no need to keep

those memories buried any longer. Carefully, plucking the little curl from the box, it stuck to the paper – and both came out. As I detached the lock of hair, I spied a few words scribbled on the back of the yellowed note. Had Byron written a poem to Allegra? Slowly turning it over, I saw it was not a poem. It was a confession.

> Forgive me, Claire. Our daughter lives . . . I could not tell you, but she survived the typhus and remains hidden for her safety.
> You will never see these words, or know that I truly loved you.
> B.

My body stiffened in shock as I read the lines once more, then again.

Allegra was still alive.

'So now you know what happened,' a deep, masculine voice said from behind.

I took in a quick, sharp breath. Slowly, I rose to my feet and turned to see Edward Trelawny standing before me. Gray-haired, with a hard-planed face, he still retained that handsome aura of the man I once knew in my youth.

My shock yielded to anger. 'Why did you send Rossetti and not come yourself?'

'I meant to arrive shortly after him, but my passage from England was delayed by rough seas.' He extended his hand toward me. 'Claire, I do not seek to justify my past behavior, but I want to explain my dishonesty—'

'You mean your lies about the past – or at least *omissions*.'

'Yes, I had secrets from you, but I am ready to confess – and I vow to remain in Italy as your protector until this web of deceit has been untangled.' He bowed his head briefly. 'But understand this . . . when I visited Byron in Greece, he showed me the obelisk sketch and related the whole story, including the part when he tore those lines out of Polidori's journal about your child – to protect you and Allegra. Byron did not think you fell down the stairs at Castle Chillon – he suspected that Ludovico di Breme pushed you.'

'Dear God.' Shock flew through me. 'I remember him. He came to visit Byron at Diodati during that summer in Geneva – and seemed nothing but a pleasant man, but Polidori's journal recorded a secret meeting with di Breme that Mary never mentioned to me. What could it mean?'

'All I know is the Italian's appearance caused Byron to be alarmed because di Breme seemed fixated on you . . . so much so, Byron asked him to leave. Byron made me promise that I would never share this knowledge with anyone, including you. After he died, the missing lines and obelisk drawing disappeared and I kept my vow, until Rossetti contacted me to say he had them both and wanted to buy your letters. I knew that I could no longer stay silent, so I asked Rossetti to come to Florence himself – and place that note under your teacup to warn you – until I could reach Italy and right this wrong from the past. I did not anticipate that his arrival would set such tragic events in motion so quickly. I know forgiveness is not possible, but will you at least hear my story?'

Staring at him in disbelief, I felt my world had shifted yet again. I had just been reconciled to put the past behind me and give up forever on the notion that Allegra had survived. But now I had proof from the one other living person who bore witness to Byron's last days.

'I cannot absolve your sins so easily, my old friend, but if you tell me all that you know, I will at least try not to condemn you,' I said as I cautiously took his hand. 'Leave nothing out.'

'I shall not,' he vowed. As our fingers intertwined, we ambled out of the garden in silent agreement and up the stairs into the light shining out from the Pitti Palace. I was about to hear the words that I had longed for most of my life.

I would finally know the truth about Allegra.